'Calm down, sweetheart,' he said, thwarting her half-hearted efforts by drawing her closer to his chest. 'It's not a problem.'

'It's difficult to calm d-down,' she sobbed against his throat. 'All I can think of is those poor people and everything they've l-lost and…and…'

She turned her head to look up at him just as he angled his to press his face against hers, and somehow, accidentally, fleetingly, their lips brushed.

He froze, unable to breathe, convinced that even his heart had stopped beating for several timeless seconds as he savoured the softness of her mouth against his for the first time.

'Daniel?' she whispered huskily, and he was utterly amazed that she hadn't immediately broken the contact between them…

Josie Metcalfe lives in Cornwall with her long-suffering husband. They have four children. When she was an army brat, frequently on the move, books became the only friends that came with her wherever she went. Now that she writes them herself she is making new friends, and hates saying goodbye at the end of a book—but there are always more characters in her head, clamouring for attention until she can't wait to tell their stories.

MIRACLE
TIMES TWO

BY
JOSIE METCALFE

First published in Great Britain 2011
by Mills & Boon, an imprint of Harlequin (UK) Limited,
Eton House, 18-24 Paradise Road, Richmond, Surrey TW9 1SR

© Josie Metcalfe 2011

ISBN: 978 0 263 21916 6

Harlequin (UK) policy is to use papers that are natural, renewable and recyclable products and made from wood grown in sustainable forests. The logging and manufacturing process conform to the legal environmental regulations of the country of origin.

Printed and bound in Great Britain
by CPI Antony Rowe, Chippenham, Wiltshire

Also by Josie Metcalfe:

A WIFE FOR THE BABY DOCTOR
SHEIKH SURGEON CLAIMS HIS BRIDE*
THE DOCTOR'S BRIDE BY SUNRISE*

Brides of Penhally Bay

Did you know these are also available as eBooks?
Visit www.millsandboon.co.uk

PROLOGUE

'PLEASE, Colin, I said no,' Jenny repeated, wondering why it seemed so hard to get the words out. It almost felt as if her tongue was tied. 'Th-thank you for bringing me home, but now it's time for you to go.'

'You don't really mean that, sweetie…not after all these weeks. Your family is just waiting to see my ring on your finger.' Colin nuzzled the side of her neck and when she could barely breathe for the pungent aftershave he was wearing, she remembered all too clearly why she'd always hated the smell of scent on a man.

She hitched her shoulder and tried to twist her head out of reach when his lips started to slide their way towards her mouth.

'Well, my family will just have to w-wait,' she said, but the words just didn't seem to emerge with the same degree of vehemence that they left her brain…and her tongue now felt as if it was too big for her mouth…and as for her eyes…it was almost impossible to focus and the lids were so heavy…

'I only w-went out with you tonight because…because it had been arranged before we…we broke up.'

'We didn't break up, sweetie,' he argued in that patronising way that managed to set her teeth on edge even when it seemed as if it came from several miles away.

'You must have had a bit too much to drink if you think that was anything more than a minor tiff. Anyway, you'll have forgotten all about it by the time you wake up in the morning with my ring on your finger...'

'*N-no!* No ring!' she said as vehemently as she could, but when she shook her head she lost her balance and nearly fell over.

'Excuse me?' said another male voice from an impossibly long way away. 'Is there a problem, here?' There was something very familiar about that new voice and she just about managed to focus on the face of the man who was able to grab her before she landed on her bottom in the hallway.

She felt curiously disconnected from everything around her, almost as if she was watching it all happening to someone else; watching as her rescuer retrieved her key and sent a clearly furious Colin away.

When her knight in shining armour swept her up into his arms she couldn't even summon up the coordination to wrap her arms around his neck, but with her head lolling on his shoulder she drew in a deep breath of soap and male skin that was oh, so familiar...trustworthy...safe.

The last fleeting memory she had was of this new but familiar man carrying her into her flat and depositing her on her bed, shoes and all, and pulling the covers over her.

CHAPTER ONE

'UM…THANK you for the other night,' Jenny said, the heat of embarrassment crawling visibly up her throat and into her face.

'No thanks necessary,' Daniel Carterton said lightly, guessing that the newest member of his team must have spent the whole of her day off working up to this apology. 'I just happened to be in the right place at the right time.' And if she believed *that*, there was a rather ornate bridge in central London on special offer.

He'd chosen his seat at the banquet honouring her father so that he could lighten the boredom of the affair by catching glimpses of Jenny across the room. That self-indulgence had been the only reason why he'd noticed the surreptitious way her companion had been topping up her glass throughout the evening. His suspicions were raised by the smug look of satisfaction on the man's face when Jenny had been less than steady on her feet when she'd finally got up from the table, but that didn't stop him from feeling almost like a stalker when he'd decided to follow them to make sure she arrived home safely.

'Do you want to answer that thing?' Daniel asked as Jenny's phone rang.

'Not in this lifetime,' she said grimly after a glance at the screen, silencing the noise with a press of a button to send the call direct to voicemail. 'And if I knew how to bar him from connecting with my mobile at all, I'd be happier still.'

'Trouble in paradise, Jennywren?' he teased, knowing he should go straight to hell for crossing his fingers that he was right. Jenny Sinclair was a genuinely lovely person who deserved a happy life with someone her equal…something he could never be. He'd been born so far on the other side of the tracks that he couldn't even hear the train from there.

And it certainly wouldn't make any difference that he'd worked his cotton socks off to become one of the youngest consultants in his field. As someone who'd only scraped into one of the lesser medical schools at his second attempt, he wouldn't stand a chance of gaining her parents' approval. Their blatant professional elitism meant that the fact that he'd been self-supporting and working crazy hours to earn every penny necessary to put himself through his training would count for nothing…even if he were ever to tell them about it. It certainly wouldn't make them look any more favourably on him for daring to look at their daughter.

So, he'd resigned himself to the fact that the only woman who could make his heart give that extra beat just by thinking about her was the one he could never have.

Well, if he was forever condemned to the role of colleague, occasional guardian angel and potential friend, he might just as well enjoy it while he could. Since Jenny had joined his unit he'd already seen a number of men make a blatant play for her, but without apparent success. Whoever was trying to ring her wasn't going to fare any better, if the expression on her face was anything to go by, but it wouldn't be long before another took his place, not with someone as special as his little Jennywren.

Except…there was something different, this time. A
shadow that hadn't been there before?

'Come on. Spill the beans,' he coaxed lightly, knowing
he was venturing into new ground. 'Which one's causing
a problem? Tell big brother all about it.'

'Big brother?' She threw him an old-fashioned look
from those fascinating hazel eyes before she pondered
darkly for a moment.

He was almost holding his breath hoping she would
confide in him when she suddenly burst into speech.

'It's Colin Fletcher,' she revealed grimly. 'He's obviously so thick-skinned that he can't take a hint…even after
you sent him off with a flea in his ear the other night.'

'That man was Colin Fletcher? As in, your father's blue-
eyed boy, Fletcher?' That *did* surprise him. He knew the
name from hospital gossip but hadn't realised the man
had been Jenny's escort that night. He was reputed to be a
born social climber from an apparently well-to-do family,
and it had been hinted that the man had his eye set firmly
on taking over Jenny's father's prestigious position at the
hospital, to say nothing of inheriting his lucrative private
practice when the great man could be persuaded to retire.
It was now blindingly obvious to Daniel that, as his son-
in-law, Fletcher would be the obvious choice, and if he
were to have a glowing recommendation from the great
man himself, it would practically make any interviews for
a replacement unnecessary.

He saw her shudder with something more than distaste
in her expression, and knowing that she was remembering
what had happened that night, every protective instinct
leapt to attention.

'He must be the slimiest, most insincere, self-serving…
weasel in the whole hospital,' she continued heatedly,
sparks almost radiating from her. 'He insisted on holding

me to the arrangement to sit at my parents' table at that big "do" the other night—in spite of the fact we weren't going out any more. He then plastered himself to my side as if we were Siamese twins, and even though I *never* have more than two glasses of wine when I go out, he must have been topping up my glass on the sly all evening, so he'd have the perfect excuse to see me home.'

'You'd already told him you wouldn't be going out with him any more?' Daniel gave her points for working out exactly what had happened at the same time as he added another item to the list of why he didn't like this Fletcher character. Top of the list was the fact that the man was the immaculately groomed poster boy for the perfect man for Jenny, unlike himself.

'I'd told him in words of one syllable that I had no inten-tion of *ever* going out with him again—and that was more than two weeks earlier—so where he got the idea that he had the right to insist on partnering me for the evening… to virtually take over control of my life…' It did Daniel's heart good to hear the anger in her voice, knowing she was coping with her near miss. The fact that she was talking about it at all was far better than bottling it up inside, and that she was comfortable using him as a confidant…

'Well, he could hardly leave you to make your own way home if you were three sheets to the wind,' he pointed out, trying to be fair even while he was rejoicing, inside, that she'd obviously seen through the little toady.

'I suppose not, even if it *was* his fault for topping up my glass without asking.'

Just the thought that the man might have set the whole thing up deliberately, that he had been within seconds of locking the two of them in Jenny's flat, was enough to have a red haze of protective fury descend over him, again, and he had to force himself to swallow the bile that rose in his throat at the very idea of this precious unattainable woman being at the mercy of that.

'I just feel so stupid that I didn't realise what he was doing until it was nearly too late. I'm just so grateful that you were there to...'

'No thanks necessary,' he said, again, hoping she wouldn't think to ask why he'd 'just happened' to be there at that time of night. He could hardly tell her he'd been watching her during the dinner and had a bad feeling about her escort's intentions, could he?

'Well, I certainly won't be getting into that sort of situation, again, even if it means suffering from dehydration,' she announced grimly. 'At least, then, I'd be sober enough to kick him out of my flat.'

'You? Kick someone out?' He raised an eyebrow and ran a teasing glance over her slender frame, mentally estimating that, while Colin wasn't particularly overweight— yet—he must be more than a head taller than she was and weigh at least half as much again. Any future escort was unlikely to be very much smaller, so her chances of overpowering an adult male were virtually nil.

'Remember, I went to those self-defence classes?' she prompted, and he almost groaned aloud at the swiftly repressed memory of the one and only time when he'd been cajoled into being her practice partner. He'd barely survived with his sanity intact after an hour of Jenny's sweetly curvaceous body climbing all over him in her attempts to pin him to the floor.

'Actually, I probably wouldn't need to do much more than twist his arm behind his back to frogmarch him to the door. He'd probably be squealing that I was damaging his hand and destroying his career,' she muttered and he couldn't help snorting with laughter.

'The mouse that roared,' he teased and tapped her on

the nose, wishing he dared linger long enough to enjoy the silky texture of her skin, but they could never have that sort of relationship.

'Hey! Who are you calling a mouse?' she demanded, smacking his hand away. 'Not that I'm not grateful for your help, but I'm sure I'd have been able to deal with him if he hadn't been topping up my glass all evening.' Then her shoulders slumped and she sighed into her coffee. 'Unfortunately, he's been bombarding me with calls, messages and texts ever since. If there was a way I could strong-arm him into leaving me alone...'

'Do you want me to have a word with him?' he offered, relishing the thought of even the slightest chance of messing with pretty boy's perfect dentistry.

'I couldn't ask you to do that,' she said, the light striking coppery sparks off her hair as she shook her head, adding firmly, 'I'm a grown woman. I should be able to deal with situations like this for myself. Anyway, he's bound to get tired of it, eventually.'

'Well, at least I can sort your phone out for you.' He held out his hand. 'Tell me the weasel's number and I'll set it up so his calls are barred.'

'How come you know how to do that?' She pushed the slender gadget across the table with a surprised expression on her face.

'Perhaps it's a boy thing,' he joked and had to duck her retribution as he accessed her contact details and pressed the relevant buttons to refuse all future calls from Colin Fletcher's mobile even as he added his own number to her phone book. 'There you are; all done. He's history.' He paused a second, but his ingrained sense of honesty forced him to admit what else he'd done. 'I've also put myself as number one on your speed dial—in place of the Chinese takeaway. So if you have any further problems...'

His offer was cut off by the insistent sound of the pager clipped to his belt and he reached for his own phone to return the call.

'This is Daniel Carterton. You paged me?' he said tersely, knowing the call was unlikely to be trivial. It very rarely was in his chosen specialty.

'One of your at-risk mums is on her way in,' the voice on the other end responded equally crisply. 'It's Aliyah Farouk. She says she's started having contractions.'

'Send someone down to A and E to bring her straight up to the unit. Whatever you do, don't let her get trapped down there by the paperwork police. I'll be there in four minutes.' He cut the connection before he swore ripely under his breath.

'Problems?' Jenny demanded, already on her feet and straightening the hem of her top and smoothing both hands over her hair to ensure it was tidy, all trace of laughter gone from her lively face.

'Apparently, Aliyah Farouk's having contractions,' he said, knowing he didn't need to say any more to Jenny for her to know the seriousness of the situation.

'Damn,' she muttered forcefully. 'We thought we'd got away with it; that she was finally on the home stretch,' she added as she followed him out of the door at a rapid clip, and sudden warmth wrapped around his heart that she'd automatically referred to the two of them as *we*. That was *something*, he consoled himself as he strode along the corridor. At least he could savour the two of them linked together as *we* in a work situation.

'If she *is* in labour, let's see if we can do something about slowing things down…at least long enough so we can do something to give the babies' lungs a chance,' he said, putting such thoughts to the back of his head with all the other things about Jenny that he had to ignore, like her surprisingly long legs that almost enabled her to keep pace with him. Instead, it was time to concentrate, setting his brain working to produce a list of possible complications that could have sparked this situation with Aliyah.

'Hi, Aliyah,' Jenny called as soon as she caught sight of their white-faced patient being wheeled swiftly into the unit by a uniformed paramedic. 'You love us so much that you couldn't stay away?'

'S-something like that,' the young woman muttered through trembling lips, then burst into noisy sobs. 'P-please help me,' she begged, clutching at Jenny's hand as tears coursed down her elegant cheeks. 'I can't lose my babies. I can't…not after everything we've gone through. You must save my little boys, even if you can't save…'

'Aliyah, no!' her darkly handsome husband interrupted fiercely before dropping to his knees in front of the wheel-chair. 'I couldn't bear to lose you,' he said before breaking into an impassioned speech in his own language.

'Jenny…' said Daniel's familiar deep voice behind her, and instantly she snapped out of her unexpected fascination with the scene in front of her.

She quickly slipped into her proper role, escorting Aliyah through to Daniel's examination room and taking her vital signs in preparation for his evaluation of the situation, but that didn't mean that she couldn't feel a residual ache of envy for the depth of love between Aliyah and her husband.

'So, let's see what's going on, then, shall we?' Daniel said as she finished adding the latest findings to Aliyah's file. 'Your blood pressure's up and so is your pulse—which is perfectly logical in a stressful situation—but they shouldn't be raising your temperature.'

Jenny had thought the same thing and had the necessary

vials ready when the decision was made to do a range of blood tests.

'In the meantime, you say you haven't been spotting but you have been experiencing pains.' His dark brows drew together thoughtfully. 'Shall we do an ultrasound to check up on your little passengers before we do anything else?'

'Please!'

'Yes, please!' The Farouks answered almost simultaneously, making everyone smile in spite of the tension in the room.

'Well, let me get you a nice big glass of water before we set everything up,' Jenny said. 'For some reason, that's the preferred method of torture used by ultrasound technicians…to make pregnant women waddle around with a baby pressing on a full bladder.' It was a joke that she often told to pregnant women in an attempt at sidetracking their thoughts, but it rarely worked very well with women as stressed-out as Aliyah Farouk, finally pregnant after a string of unexplained spontaneous abortions.

This whole side of the unit was relatively new to Jenny, who'd spent several years working with the most fragile of their premature babies under the unit's director, Josh Weatherby. Then Daniel had joined the team, the focus of his attention being the at-risk mothers and babies—those who needed his special skills if they were to have a hope of a successful pregnancy—and she'd found herself fascinated by the new field.

Of course, as soon as word had gone round that he was good-looking, heterosexual and single, there had been much laughter among the existing staff about the sudden influx of nurses wanting to join his specialist side of the unit even if it meant undergoing further training, but for Jenny, that had just been a particularly delicious bonus.

She had decided to take advantage of the opportunity

when it was offered, as a way to step back from the constant minute-by-minute stress of caring for babies who could stop breathing at any moment, or suffer from a catastrophic intracranial bleed with very little warning, or develop necrotising enterocolitis, or any one of dozens of other complications.

She hadn't realised until it was too late that it could be every bit as stressful caring for the pregnant women referred to the unit and the children they were fighting to carry, especially as she grew to know them over the weeks of their pregnancy. Anyway, by the time she'd realised it, she was hooked on the job and the delight of working with someone as focused and professional as Daniel. The fact that he also had a wicked sense of humour and was one of the best-looking and sexiest members of staff, causing a spike in her pulse rate whenever he entered a room, had absolutely nothing to do with it.

Aliyah Farouk had been one of the first patients she had met in the at-risk category, and she'd immediately warmed to the woman, feeling an empathy for her desire to continue with her legal work as long as possible. It had been during a wait for an earlier ultrasound that Aliyah had confided the details of her battle with her ultra-traditional parents to be allowed to study the law that had struck a chord with Jenny's own battles after her decision to become a nurse rather than follow her parents' preferred route as a third-generation doctor.

'Let's see if we can get a clear picture, yet,' the ultrasound technician said a while later as she squirted a small mound of clear pale blue gel on the neat swell of Aliyah's belly. 'And there's absolutely no truth to the rumour that we keep that gel in the fridge so we can shock the baby into running around.'

A shoulder pressed firmly against hers as Jenny craned

her neck to see the shadowy image appearing on the screen and she didn't need to glance at the lean muscled body or draw in the mixture of soap, hospital laundry starch and warm man to know that it was Daniel standing beside her. Her galloping pulse had already told her that.

'Well, baby one is still definitely there,' the technician said as she gestured towards the patterns of dark and light that differentiated between foetus and the surrounding water and maternal tissues. 'And there's a second very healthy heart there, too. Listen.'

The rapid patter of two foetal heartbeats, one after the other, filled the room and one of the little creatures suddenly seemed to react to the fact that they were all intruding on what should have been a private place, almost seeming to wave a fist at them.

'All right, little ones,' the technician chuckled as she tapped the necessary buttons to record the scan and silence the Doppler. 'We've seen that you're both safe and sound in there, so we'll go away and leave you in peace, now.'

Aliyah burst into noisy sobs of relief and Jenny was certain that there was a suspicious gleam in her stoic husband's eye, too, as he cradled her dark head against his shoulder.

'So, if there is nothing wrong with the babies, why is Aliyah having pains?' he demanded, apparently only allowing his fear to show now that his wife couldn't see his face. 'Is there something wrong with *her*?'

'That's what we're trying to find out with the tests we've taken,' Daniel explained calmly. 'It shouldn't be long before we have the first of the results back.'

'Now that the ultrasound's been done, it would be a good time to do some urine tests, too,' Jenny suggested. 'Aliyah's probably desperate for the bathroom by now.'

'Good idea,' Daniel agreed. 'And then, could we find

her a comfortable place to rest until we know what's going on?'

'You think I need to stay in hospital?' The idea clearly horrified her. 'You think it's something so serious that I can't go home?'

'I've no idea at the moment,' he said and Jenny registered that, although she hadn't known Daniel for very long, in that time he'd never been anything less than absolutely honest with a patient. 'But it would be a good idea if you tried to stay as calm as possible until we get all the results, if only for the sake of your blood pressure. It would be better for the babies, too.'

'And for me,' her harried husband added.

Jenny stayed until Aliyah was as settled as she was going to be in one of the side rooms closest to Daniel's office, adding her voice to the young woman's when she urged her husband to go back to the important business meeting he'd been called out of.

'Your wife and baby are safe here,' she pointed out logically. 'They're surrounded by doctors and nurses, and if it's a problem caused by some sort of infection, the antibiotics we've given her will already be starting to do their job.'

'I have this mask to hand if the pains return,' Aliyah added as she held up the clear plastic face mask attached to the Entonox. 'And anyway, this is a room where I can have my mobile switched on, so I can call you or receive your calls whenever you wish.'

It took several minutes of reassurance and then several more supplying the suddenly tearful woman with tissues after her husband left before Jenny was free to set off in search of Daniel.

She found him just as he was reaching for a piece of paper being spat out by the printer.

'Please, tell me that's the preliminary report from the

lab and it's just a simple waterworks infection; bladder or kidney, I don't mind which, just as long as there's nothing wrong with the pregnancy,' she demanded and was rewarded with a broad grin.

'Your every wish is my command,' he said with a flourishing bow, then handed her the paper to add to Aliyah's file. 'Obviously, there hasn't been time to isolate the particular bug causing the problem, but as we put her on trimethoprim in the interim…'

'She could have relief from her symptoms within an hour,' Jenny finished for him.

'Within one to four hours,' he temporised. 'It would probably be quicker relief with ciprofloxacin, but that's not so good for the pregnancy.'

He went on to run through the progress on several other cases, but Jenny suddenly knew that he was feeling every bit as relieved and delighted with the prospects for Aliyah's pregnancy as she was.

The realisation was so unexpected that, for a moment, she completely lost track of what Daniel was saying.

Was she just imagining that she could read his feelings, or was she actually beginning to be able to see beyond the cheerfully professional persona he showed the world?

It was always unlikely that one person could be that unfailingly even-tempered and still be human, and that opened up a whole new world of possibilities in the mystery of the gorgeous specimen of masculinity that was Daniel Carterton. Possibilities such as, if his smiles *were* a camouflage for other, deeper thoughts, was he hiding secrets…and if so, what sort of secrets?

Not that it would ever be something dark—such as Colin's underhanded ploy to get her alone when he obviously cared very little for her other than the fact of who her father was.

No. If Daniel had secrets they would be...what?

'What?' the man in question echoed, snapping her out of her crazy thoughts and into the real world and the recognition that she had absolutely no idea what he was talking about.

'What?' she repeated, feeling stupid and horribly afraid that she was going to blush.

'That's what I asked you,' he said with a puzzled frown. 'You were just standing there, staring at me as if you were trying to unravel the secrets of the universe on the end of my nose.'

She closed her eyes for a second, grateful that at least he hadn't realised it was those gorgeous deep blue eyes and their unfairly long lashes she'd been gazing at, or the rogue curl of dark hair curving forward onto his forehead as he worked his way through the basket of correspondence waiting for his attention.

One envelope contained a photograph of a perfect set of twins, obviously identical, even down to the slightly cross expression on their faces, and she couldn't help chuckling.

'Anybody you know?' she asked.

'Their mother was one of the earliest patients I saw when I came to work here—before you joined the unit,' he said and reached for a manila folder standing beside his computer to slip the photo inside with what looked like quite a few others.

'Are they all your babies in there?' she demanded, holding out a hand for the folder before she thought how intrusive he might find it.

'Sometimes parents send me a picture to let me know their babies have arrived safely,' he said, upending the folder in the middle of his desk to reveal dozens of babies, from the smallest, wrinkliest preemie to some that looked to be at least three months old when they were born.

'Why have you got all these hidden away?' she demanded as she spread them out across his paperwork. 'These should all be on display somewhere.'

'On display?' He looked as if the idea had never crossed his mind. 'Why?'

'For reassurance,' she said impatiently. 'You deal with at-risk mums and babies, so you have a far higher mortality rate than an ordinary Obs and Gynae department. Most parents–to-be come here expecting the worst and it would be so good if the first thing they saw when they came into your room is a whole array of photos of the healthy happy babies you've helped on their way...far more babies than the number that *don't* survive,' she pointed out.

His attempt at a response was cut short by the strident ring of the telephone and she'd only taken a couple of steps towards the door to afford him some privacy for the call when the sudden tension in his voice stopped her in her tracks.

'When? Where? How long ago?' he snapped out in short order. 'Well, find out and ring me back as soon as you do. Have you notified Josh Weatherby?'

With the mention of the senior consultant a shiver of dread ran up Jenny's spine, every hair standing up on end in its wake.

Whatever it was, this did not sound good; not if it involved the man who took charge of all the seriously premature babies or those with peri-natal problems.

'What's happened?' she asked as soon as he took the phone away from his ear.

Her words collided with his as he rapped out, 'There's been an accident, right outside the hospital.'

'Not one of *our* mums,' she pleaded, but the grim expression on his face was enough to confirm the bad news.

'Sheelagh Griffin,' he said, already tapping to access the young woman's file on the computer. 'Apparently, she started spotting heavily and cramping this morning, so her husband insisted on driving her in. He hit a pedestrian as he was turning in through the gates and smashed their car into one of the granite pillars.'

'Do you need me to come down with you?' It was a given that he would be going down to A and E to speed the young woman's admission to the unit, otherwise she could be caught up in the nightmare of paperwork until it was too late to do anything for the precious babies.

'Stay up here, for now,' he said after only a moment's hesitation. 'I can call you down if I need to, but you'll be my eyes and ears up here while I'm away.'

Jenny was immensely flattered that he would already think her competent for such a responsibility. She had done extra training for this new position but she was a nurse rather than a doctor—much to her parents' enduring disappointment.

'Let me know if you want me to get anything organised,' she said, startled to realise that what she'd really wanted to say was *Hurry back.*

And how stupid is that? she berated herself before he was even out of sight. She and Daniel didn't have that sort of relationship, and there was very little chance that they ever would. After all, no matter what her parents' narrow-minded view was of people who had risen to the top in spite of starting off at one of the less elite medical schools, Daniel was something of a high-flier, and as such, was stratospherically beyond the reach of a humble nurse, no matter how well trained and good at her job.

Anyway, hadn't Daniel categorised their relationship just a short while ago when he'd invited her to *'tell big brother'* about her troubles?

Colleague…little sister…*friend*, perhaps? She might slot into several niches in Daniel's life, but there was very little chance that he would be interested in seeing her in a role that she was only now beginning to realise might be the one she really wanted.

The phone rang stridently at her elbow, snapping her out of her pointless reflections and doubling her pulse rate with the expectation that she would hear Daniel's voice when she answered it. It was a complete letdown to realise that the caller had simply been connected to the wrong department.

'Jenny?' Daniel's voice behind her had her whirling to face him, the first of at least a dozen questions on the tip of her tongue until she saw his face.

'Daniel? What's happened?' she demanded, automatically reaching out to take his arm. 'Are you ill?' He looked positively grim, and in the short time he'd been away from the department, his face had somehow become hollow-looking, his eyes filled with shadows.

'I was too late to do anything to slow down Sheelagh's labour,' he said bluntly, and she could hear the same defeated tone that always emerged in his voice whenever something happened to one of their special babies, but this time there was something more, something infinitely darker.

CHAPTER TWO

'ARE the babies still alive? Have they gone to Josh's unit?'

Even babies that premature were often born alive and a few of them actually pulled through, albeit with a legacy of permanent disabilities, but it was an outside chance that they would have survived anything other than a Caesarean birth.

'One is.' Daniel grimaced, silently, the brilliant colour of his dancing blue eyes strangely flat. 'I've admitted Sheelagh into the isolation room overnight. I told her it was in case of complications, but they both know it's just a matter of time before...'

She nodded her understanding even as she thought that they really should think of a better name for the little suite at the furthest end of the unit. Apparently, that little area had been one of the arrangements Daniel had instigated within the first few days of his appointment—a place where mothers who had lost their babies could stay for monitoring and treatment without fear that their devastation would be made worse by the sights and sounds of pregnant women or healthy newborn babies all around them.

'Did it happen because of the accident?' Jenny demanded, something about the tension surrounding him like an electrical field warning her that there was worse news to come.

'My guess is that one of the babies died *in utero* and that triggered a spontaneous abortion of both foetuses.' He sank heavily into the chair and came to rest with his hands tightly linked together on the array of happy photos still spread over the inevitable pile of papers in front of him. He gazed blankly at them for several endless seconds while she fought the urge to go to him and throw her arms around him, to cradle his head against her and ask if there was anything she could do.

'The person they ran down was Aliyah's husband,' he announced rawly, and his devastated expression rocked her back on her heels.

'Dear Lord,' she gasped, sinking heavily onto the edge of the nearest chair when her legs refused to support her. 'Is he...?' She couldn't bring herself to say the word, but she didn't need to for him to know what she was asking.

'He's in theatre. Depressed skull fracture, punctured lung, broken leg...you name it, he's got it,' he listed grimly and she felt her eyes widen with each additional injury on the list.

'But he's still alive?' she pleaded anxiously.

'For the moment,' he agreed and it only took the tone of his voice to know that the prognosis wasn't good.

Her heart sank like a stone. 'What are you going to tell Aliyah?' The image in her head of how tenderly the injured man had been supporting his wife less than an hour ago was so clear that it was almost painful.

'How on earth was he injured so badly?' she demanded on a sudden surge of anger for the destruction of such a perfect couple made even more tragic by the fact they were finally expecting the babies they both wanted so badly.

'Did he forget where he was and step out into the traffic, or...?'

'Apparently, the Griffiths' car went out of control and mounted the pavement at the entrance to the hospital. He was slammed against one of the pillars and trapped.'

Jenny winced as she imagined a human head coming into contact with that impressive construction of unforgiving Cornish granite.

'And I have absolutely *no* idea what I'm going to say to Aliyah,' he said finally, his voice as rough as gravel. 'She's still shaky after that scare with the baby and we're waiting for the antibiotics to do their thing. I don't know whether I should hold off telling her in the hopes that he comes out of surgery with some sort of positive prognosis, or whether I should go to her straight away in case she needs to prepare herself to say her final farewell while he's still alive.'

'Or at least given a semblance of life by various machinery,' she muttered, feeling sickened by the awful possibility.

How would *she* feel if she were in the same position?

Would she rather know, immediately, that the man she loved had been terribly injured and was not expected to live, and have to agonise for hours imagining what was going on in theatre? Or would she prefer to receive the news after every effort had been made to repair the damage?

'If she weren't pregnant...' Daniel muttered and she knew he was weighing up exactly the same options and trying to balance their patient's right to know against the increased risk to her pregnancy such a shock might cause.

A sudden unearthly scream from further along the corridor sent all the hairs up on the back of Jenny's neck.

'What on *earth*...?' She whirled and took off out of

Daniel's office at a fast clip, almost colliding with a young nurse catapulting out of Aliyah Farouk's room.

'Nooo!' The unearthly scream sounded again, then was replaced by a wail that degenerated into inconsolable weeping.

'What's going on here?' Daniel demanded, glaring fiercely at the shocked-looking nurse.

'I don't know, s-sir!' The poor girl's teeth were almost chattering. 'Sh-she was trying to phone her husband's work to leave a message and they said he hadn't arrived. S-so she said she was going to try his mobile phone and…and…'

Jenny winced as she put two and two together. It didn't take much to imagine the scene in a busy A and E, especially as her husband's clothing would have been summarily cut off his body to enable swift access to his injuries. Keeping track of his mobile phone would have been a low priority, everything being stuffed into the same bag for later retrieval.

It was all too easy to imagine the junior member of staff detailed to take charge of yet another patient's belongings to think it was a good idea to tell a seriously injured patient's wife that she needed to come to the hospital as soon as possible.

'Okay, Joanne. Go and get yourself a cup of tea and don't come back until you've stopped shaking. Let someone know where you're going,' Jenny said.

'Th-thank you,' she stammered, but Jenny was already following Daniel into the room, shutting the door firmly against any intrusion.

She was just in time to see him reach out to the keening woman and gasped in disbelief when Aliyah turned on him like a rabid dog, her eyes wild and her fingers stiffly curved as though ready to rip him to shreds.

'No, Aliyah, no,' Daniel said, his deep voice almost

crooning as, far from backing away, he stepped straight
into the danger zone and wrapped a consoling arm around
her shoulders. 'Gently. Gently,' he said. 'This is not good
for the babies. Think about those precious babies.' His
words were almost hypnotic in their gentle rise and fall,
but it took several racking moments before Aliyah's devastation would allow her to hear what he was saying.

Suddenly, she flung herself into Daniel's arms and he
had to ease himself onto the side of the bed to support her
weight as she sobbed, clearly broken-hearted.

'*Why?*' she wailed at intervals, but there was obviously
no answer for the randomness of chance. If her husband
had decided not to go back to his office, or if he had decided to leave even a couple of minutes earlier, this would
not have happened.

It was only when she finally drew back from Daniel's
comforting hold and looked up at him from tear-swollen
eyes she demanded, 'Why did he have to die before he
could even see our sons?' that Jenny understood the enor-
mity of her devastation.

For a moment, she wondered whether the information
was true. Then she put her rational head on and recognised
that the person who had answered the phone in A and E
was unlikely to have more up-to-date news than Daniel.

Still, she reached for the phone and pressed the relevant
numbers.

'Theatres,' said a crisply efficient voice when the call
was answered.

'This is Jenny Sinclair calling on behalf of Daniel Carterton,' she announced. 'Can you give me an update on Mr
Farouk's surgery? His wife's a patient in our unit.'

'Oh, no!' the voice exclaimed, instantly sympathetic,
then, 'Just give me a minute to check,' but Jenny wasn't
worried about a moment or two's delay. It might give

Aliyah time to comprehend the fact that her husband hadn't died at the scene of the accident, as she seemed to believe.

'Surgery's still ongoing,' the voice reported in her ear while she watched Daniel try to calm his patient enough to listen to what he needed to explain. 'There are three of them working on him at the moment—a thoracic surgeon, an orthopod and a neurosurgeon. They said they've managed to stop the bleeding but there's still a long way to go before they'll know anything definite. Do you want someone to phone with updates?'

'Please,' Jenny confirmed. 'Updates would be good,' and she put the phone down.

'He's still alive?' Aliyah breathed with tremulous disbelief, her thick dark lashes clumped by tears. 'Please, tell me he's still alive.'

'So far,' Jenny cautioned, stepping close enough to take the hand the young woman held out to her. She squeezed it reassuringly between both of hers as she paraphrased the information she'd just been given. 'So far, they've managed to stop him bleeding, but that's only the first step.'

'What else do they have to do? When will I be able to see him?' She flipped back the covers and started to slide her feet over the side of the bed. 'Please, can I go to him? I need to be with him.'

Daniel had to step in with a doctor's authority before they could persuade their patient that there was absolutely no point in trailing through the hospital only to have to sit in a surgical waiting room.

'We'll probably receive news, here, before you would, there,' Daniel pointed out. 'Jenny has arranged for someone in the surgical department to phone through updates as soon as there is anything to tell us.'

'You promise?' Her dark eyes flicked frantically from

one to the other. 'You will tell me as soon as you hear anything?'

'I'll promise if you'll promise, too,' Daniel said firmly, then pointed to the figures on the monitor panel. 'You must lie back and relax and concentrate on bringing your pulse and blood pressure down, for your babies' sakes. Do you think your husband would forgive himself if worrying about him damaged your sons?'

The rest of her shift seemed interminable and it almost felt to Jenny as if they were all holding their breath while they waited for news of the surgery.

The report that Aliyah's husband had survived the removal of several large shards of bone from his brain and that the plate of skull they'd removed to access them would not be replaced until some of the swelling had gone down was the final part in the lengthy process.

Not that surviving the complex operations would guarantee the patient's survival, and there was still an extremely long way to go before they would even begin to know how much permanent damage his brain had suffered in the impact and its aftermath.

'Are you as exhausted as I am?' Jenny demanded as she emerged from the locker room still sliding her arms into the sleeves of her jacket to find Daniel performing almost exactly the same task as he walked towards her.

'Probably,' he grumbled. 'And it's not as if the day was unusually busy.'

In fact, the unit had been relatively quiet, beyond the usual round of clinics and assessments. Of course, there was an almost electric buzz in the air every time the phone rang, with everyone seeming to hold their breath in case it was news about Sheelagh Griffin's desperately struggling baby or the outcome of Faz Farouk's lengthy surgery. It was always that way when one of 'their' patients had bad news, and in a unit that saw the highest-risk patients, they saw more sadness than most.

This seemed somehow different, almost as if the whole world was waiting to hear the outcome. And still the tiny baby clung to life as though oblivious to the fact that his fight was doomed to failure, while Aliyah Farouk waited impatiently to be given permission to go to her husband's side.

'I never realised that tension could be so draining,' she said as she automatically fell into step beside him, both of them heading towards the exit after their brief detour to glimpse the tiny scrap that was barely as long as her hand. 'But I suppose that when everything revs into high gear every time the phone rings...'

'And your body gets flooded with adrenaline in anticipation of news,' he added.

'So your pulse and respiration speed up, causing you to burn up so many calories that you feel completely limp and empty even before the situation resolves itself.'

'So, you're saying that you're about to collapse with lack of nourishment and are in imminent need of sustenance?' he asked and she was grateful that he'd changed the topic to something so mundane and normal.

'How did you guess?' Jenny pulled a face as she rubbed a hand over the noises coming from her stomach. 'I know it's not the best thing nutritionally, but I think I'm going to get a takeaway, for speed.'

'I could do *tagliatelli carbonara*, if you're interested?' he offered tentatively and she blinked in surprise, then wondered if, like her, he didn't want to be alone with his thoughts just yet.

She had to squash the bubble of excitement that started to swell inside her at the idea that she'd be spending some off-duty time with him. After all, it hadn't been so long ago that he'd let her know he saw her as more of a little sister than an attractive woman.

'How long would I have to wait to eat?' she demanded, concentrating on looking suspicious. 'Is that a crafty way of getting me to do the shopping so you'll have the ingredients to cook?'

'I'm mortally wounded that you could think me so devious!' he complained as he stepped aside to allow her to exit the automatic doors first. 'When have I ever given you cause to think that I'm anything other than honest and straightforward?'

His teasing words died away as she came to a halt, her way blocked by a darkly scowling Colin Fletcher.

'There's something wrong with your phone,' he announced bluntly. 'I've been trying to ring you all day to tell you I'd be picking you up at the end of your shift.'

Jenny swallowed hard, tempted to close her eyes tightly to pretend that the obnoxious man wasn't standing there, clearly unconcerned that he was about to cause a scene in front of goodness knew how many colleagues, patients and visitors.

'There's nothing wrong with my phone,' she said quietly, not certain whether she was glad to have Daniel's silent presence at her back or embarrassed that he was a witness to the result of her stupidity in ever agreeing to go out with Colin in the first place.

'There *must* be something wrong because I haven't been able to get through,' Colin argued with a pointed glance at his watch then a disparaging look at her favourite pair of well-worn jeans. 'You'll need to get yourself tidied up enough to go somewhere decent like the Pastorale. I'd better give you a lift to your flat or you're not going to have enough time to make a good job of it.'

The classy French restaurant that had opened recently at the top end of the high street had quickly made a name for its elegant ambiance and superb cuisine, but it certainly wasn't the place she wanted to go after a stressful day like today…nor was Colin the company she'd ever choose.

'Thank you for the invitation, Colin,' she said, so perfectly politely that even the pickiest manners maven couldn't have found fault, 'but I'm really not in the mood for—'

'Not in the *mood*!' he interrupted angrily. 'Do you real-ise how exclusive Pastorale is; how hard it was to organise a reservation at such short notice so I could stage the ro-mantic—?' He stopped himself suddenly, almost as if he'd said more than he'd intended, then continued, sounding angrier than ever. 'And you're standing there saying you're not in the *mood*?'

'Excuse me.' It was Daniel's turn to interrupt and Jenny almost giggled when the unexpectedness of it left Colin with his mouth agape.

It was tempting to allow the strong silent man at her back to take over for her, but she'd never been one to back down from a battle that was important to her, and this one definitely qualified.

'Colin, there's no point in trying to browbeat me into going for a meal with you, because it isn't going to happen,' she said firmly.

'Well, I'd have been able to get hold of you to arrange it properly earlier on today if your phone had been working,' he began again, but this time she interrupted him herself.

'There is absolutely nothing wrong with my phone,' she declared. 'I've already told you that I won't go out with you, several times, in fact. So I've had my phone pro-grammed to refuse any of your calls. Now, if you'll excuse me, there's an enormous plate of *tagliatelli carbonara* with my name on it and I'm starving. Goodnight, Colin.'

Her knees felt rather wobbly as she forced herself to stride briskly past the man, but the matching echo of Daniel's feet following close behind fanned the spark of defiance that kept her chin in the air and bolstered the confidence that her nemesis would never know how uncertain she'd been that she could cope with such an uncomfortable confrontation.

'So there's an *enormous* plate of *carbonara* with your name on it, is there?' Daniel mused as he lengthened his stride to catch up with her as they set off across the vast car park to the other side of the hospital grounds. 'I'm not certain that I've got enough ingredients for that. Perhaps we *should* detour to do a bit of shopping, just to be sure.'

Jenny had no idea why his teasing should suddenly make her feel like crying and laughing aloud at the same time, but it took a real effort not to do either...or both.

'*No* shopping,' she decreed imperiously, warmed beyond words that she had such a friend and overwhelmingly grateful for his ready sense of humour. 'I need food *now*!'

A leisurely hour later they were both coming to the end of plates full of perfectly cooked *tagliatelli* smothered in the most delicious creamy sauce, and Daniel's light-hearted banter had temporarily managed to push their concerns about their patients to the back of their minds. It had also all but banished the memory of that unfortunate scene at the entrance to the hospital's main Reception. In fact, she was feeling so relaxed that that she wasn't sure she was going to be able to summon up the energy to walk to her own flat, and there was a real danger that she would fall asleep where she sat if she stayed much longer.

Regretfully, she began to fish under the table for the shoes she'd kicked off soon after she'd arrived, trying to find the words to thank him, not only for the delicious meal but also for standing by her while she faced Colin down, yet still allowing her to deal with the situation herself.

She was just drawing a breath to bring the evening to a close when his mobile phone began to vibrate its way across the centre of the table.

'Carterton.' His brisk response told her she wasn't going to have to eavesdrop on a one-sided private call and the resigned expression that came over his face was enough to tell her that Sheelagh Griffin's baby had lost his fight.

'Poor woman,' she whispered, her heart heavy for the couple who would have to start the whole IVF process all over again if they were ever to have the family they wanted.

Before Daniel could comment his phone was ringing again, but this time the shocked way his eyes widened told her the news he was getting was totally unexpected and it wasn't good.

Listening in on a call that largely consisted of one-word questions was both frustrating and frightening, especially when she saw the regret fill his face.

'What?' she demanded as soon as the call ended. 'What's happened? Oh, no! Is it Aliyah? How bad is it?'

He raked his fingers through his thick dark hair and swore ripely, something she very rarely heard him do.

'It's not Aliyah,' he said but before she could let the relief flood through her he added, 'it's her husband. He coded in ICU and it took five tries to get him back.'

Jenny felt close to tears when she remembered what a lovely caring man Faz was and how concerned about Aliyah and their baby. 'How long was his heart stopped? Do they know why?'

'They've taken him back to theatre. There's blood building up in the pericardium that's stopping the heart from working properly. It nearly stopped it permanently.'

'Surely they would have checked for other sources of bleeding when they were retrieving the bone fragments from the broken ribs and sorting out the collapsed lung?'

Daniel's expression was wry because they both knew that such things could be missed when a patient presented with so many life-threatening injuries at once, especially if the damage was small enough to make any bleed insig-nificant amongst all the other gore.

Sadly, she realised that their almost idyllic evening was over—the outside world back with a vengeance—and suddenly her exhaustion made everything more than she could bear—the situation with Colin and their embarrass-ing confrontation, the worry that Aliyah might be losing her longed-for babies, Sheelagh Griffin's accident right at the hospital's gates and the loss of both of her precious babies. Now this! The horrible events still seemed to be piling up.

With barely a second's warning her breath caught in her throat and her eyes burned as they filled with tears.

'Oh, Daniel,' she wailed, then whirled towards his door, wanting nothing more than to escape before he saw them start to stream down her face.

'Hey!' He caught her arm as she fumbled with the lock on the front door and swung her gently around. 'Are you going without your shoes?'

The concerned frown pleating his forehead was the final straw, releasing the first sob from the dammed-up agony in her throat, and when he pulled her into the sanctuary of his arms the floodgates burst.

'Shh!' Daniel soothed helplessly as he awkwardly patted her back, realising wryly that, for all his extensive education, he had no more idea of how to deal with a crying woman than any other man.

And the fact that a large part of his brain was taken up with registering just how perfect Jenny felt in his arms wasn't something he had any control over, either.

She was such an energetic person with such a lively personality that it was all too easy to forget just how slender she was, especially when she was swathed in a shapeless uniform or several bulky layers of off-duty clothing—one of the down sides of spending her working days in a heated building.

Now that he had her wrapped in his arms he realised that she was more than a head shorter than he was, easily able to burrow herself into the angle under his chin as she clung to him.

The hand that started stroking her back traced the perfect curve of her spine from the silky hair at the base of her skull all the way down to the top of her jeans, and he was almost certain that, had he tried, he could have wrapped both hands completely around her waist, fingertip to fingertip.

And as for her legs, those deceptively long legs, one of which he was bracketing with his own as she leaned against him, sparking his imagination to fill with images of how they would feel without the layers of fabric separating them, how it would feel if they were both naked with those endless legs wrapped around his waist as he...

'Oh, Daniel, I'm sorry,' she whimpered against his throat and he had to swallow a groan as the puffs of moist warmth on his bare skin ratcheted his pulse still higher even as he tried to remind himself that he was supposed to be supporting and comforting her, not wasting his time imagining impossible scenarios in which...

'There's nothing to be sorry for,' he growled, hoping

she couldn't hear the way his voice betrayed the effect she was having on him.

'I sh-shouldn't be falling apart all over you,' she hic-cupped. 'It's not fair to you to have to m-mop me up.'

'You let me worry about that,' he reassured her, even as he tried to push to the back of his brain all the other things he'd be willing to do for her. To her. With her. 'Everyone needs a friend they can let the barriers down with, other-wise we'd all go crazy in a high-stress job like ours.'

He rested his cheek briefly on the crown of her head just long enough to draw in the fresh scent of the shampoo she'd used earlier mixed with the indefinable something that belonged to no one but his little Jennywren.

'It never seems to get to you,' she complained. 'Even when you came back up to tell us about Sheelagh Griffin's babies.' The thought sent her off into renewed sobs and he realised that, as it didn't look as if she was going to be fit to leave any time soon, it was time to make them both more comfortable.

She was weeping so hard that she was probably almost unaware that he'd half-led, half-carried her back into his living room. In fact, she only reacted when he lowered himself into the corner of his oversized settee and tried to settle her on his lap.

'Daniel, no,' she objected, floundering in her attempts at getting her feet on the floor. 'You don't have to do this. It's not… You can't want… I shouldn't…'

'Calm down, sweetheart,' he said, thwarting her half-hearted efforts by drawing her closer to his chest. 'It's not a problem.' Well, that was a blatant lie for a start, because having her squirming on his lap was quickly becoming a big problem, and if she squirmed much more, she would discover just how big.

'It's difficult to calm d-down,' she sobbed against his

throat. 'All I can think of is those poor people and every-thing they've l-lost and…and…'

She turned her head to look up at him just as he angled his to press his face against hers and somehow, acciden-tally, fleetingly, their lips brushed.

He froze, unable to breathe, convinced that even his heart had stopped beating for several timeless seconds as he savoured the softness of her mouth against his for the first time.

'Daniel?' she whispered huskily, and while he was ut-terly amazed that she hadn't immediately broken the con-tact between them, he was intimately aware that he could taste the salt of her tears.

The last thing he wanted was to draw back, afraid of what he would see in her eyes. Shock? Rejection? Or worse, disgust if she thought he was taking advantage of her emotional state?

In the end it was Jenny who moved just the few inches that would allow them to see each other's expressions, and the wide-eyed wonder on her face as her gaze flicked from his eyes to his mouth and back again jolted his heart into double time.

'Jenny?' It sounded more like a growl than a question and he wasn't really sure what he was trying to ask her, but to his everlasting relief she seemed to take it as an invitation.

'Please,' she whispered as she angled her head and leant forwards just far enough to stroke her lips over his…once… twice… 'Please, Daniel,' she said again as she wreathed her arms around his neck, this time pressing not only her lips against his but the whole of her body, too. 'Please, Daniel. I need you,' she begged breathlessly before she plunged them both headlong into the kind of kiss he'd been dreaming of ever since he'd met the tantalising woman... only better.

CHAPTER THREE

DANIEL woke to find Jenny still in his arms and an unexpected image suddenly sprang into his mind.

He'd been sent to stay with his grandfather one summer, and every morning he'd been woken by the elderly man's favourite cockerel that used to fly to the top of a big wooden gatepost and crow.

Now, for the first time in his life, Daniel knew exactly how Ruben the Rhode Island Red rooster had felt. After the night he and Jenny had just spent together, he almost believed he could leap to the top of the roof to shout to the world how good he was feeling.

Except…

Except there was a very honest part of him that was kicking himself for his loss of control. Guilt was telling him that he should have been stronger when Jenny had been falling apart; that he should have been able to comfort her without succumbing to the desire that had been building in him ever since he'd met her.

And while he was relishing the fact that he had this precious time with her in his arms, he was dreading the moment when she woke, afraid he would see the same expression in her eyes that she'd had when she'd spoken about Colin's attempt to take advantage of her.

It was easy to push that thought to the back of his mind

when he was looking down at her curled up trustingly at his side, her head nestled into his shoulder and her forehead against the curve of his neck. He couldn't think of a more arousing way to wake up than with the warmth of her breath soughing over his chest, ruffling and teasing the hairs and tightening his nipples into hard points that were begging for more of her attention.

Even then, with the evidence all around him, the tumbled bedding, the scattered clothing, the musky, totally arousing scent that was partly his and partly hers…he still could hardly believe that it had really happened.

It wasn't simply the fact that it had happened at all that had him reeling, either; it was the sheer scale of it that had been enough to blow his mind for the next millennium or so.

That hadn't been the Jenny he had thought he was coming to know at the hospital. *She* was the calm, caring, concerned professional who could be counted on to go the extra mile for every one of their patients with sympathy and tact. It hadn't been the off-duty Jenny, either; the cheerful, friendly young woman with a welcoming smile for everyone even while surrounded by an indefinable air that sometimes came across almost as naïveté.

No, the Jenny he'd discovered last night had been a complete revelation; an unbelievably arousing combination of uncertainty and boldness; of alternating shyness and daring that had rendered him speechless and breathless and utterly captivated.

Making love with her had been more—*much* more— than he'd ever imagined, and it was something he'd be delighted to repeat on a daily basis far beyond the foreseeable future but…

He drew in a controlled breath as he fought down a feeling of dread.

Yes, it had been, without exception, the most spectacular night of his life, and hers, too, if her eager reaction was anything to go by, but would he still be basking in this contented glow thinking the night's pleasure had been worth it if it meant he'd lost her friendship?

He'd already admitted to himself the fact that there was little chance of anything permanent between them, but he'd hoped that at least in the time they spent together they could be friends as well as colleagues. Had he ruined that, now?

A glance at the alarm clock told him that it was still early. Too early to get ready for work. In fact, it was early enough for a leisurely repeat session that he was craving more with every second, even though he knew he couldn't have it.

He should leave the bed, *now*. Leave her in the hopes that she wouldn't be too angry that he'd taken advantage of her distress.

His mobile phone suddenly buzzed into life, the vibrate function making it rattle noisily on the chest of drawers beside the bed.

Daniel was glad that at least he'd had the presence of mind to switch off the noisy ring tone. Now all he had to do was silence the wretched thing quickly enough that it didn't wake the sleeping woman in his arms. It was going to take a while longer before he'd be ready to face her.

But before he could untangle an arm to reach for the infernal gadget, her eyes flicked open, their hazel irises glowing with golden fire as they gazed straight up into his.

The phone buzzed again and she glanced fleetingly at it before her eyes returned to his, the slumberous expression in them almost making him groan aloud as his body started to respond.

'Are you going to answer that?' she prompted with a hint of a grin. 'It doesn't sound as if they're going to give up.'

The impish curve of lips that had met his own time and time again during the night was almost enough to make him forget his name, but there was no way he could ignore his phone when there were vulnerable patients relying on him.

'Car—' he began then had to clear his throat before he could continue, the husky tone far more suited to the bedroom than his professional persona. 'Carterton,' he announced crisply on his second attempt, mentally switching gears. The last thing he needed to be thinking about was bedrooms when he was taking a call from the hospital.

'Hello. I'm sorry to disturb you so early, Dr Carterton, but you wouldn't happen to know where Jenny Barber might be?'

'What?' He could feel the unexpected heat of a blush searing up his throat and into his face, hardly able to believe that the woman in question was still curled sleepily against him as if she was totally unaware that the two of them were wrapped around each other, completely naked.

'Oh, I'm *so* sorry!' the voice on the other end of the line exclaimed. 'That must have come out of left field, especially this early in the morning. And I didn't even tell you who I am…and I probably woke you up, too. I'm *so* sorry!'

'You didn't wake me,' Daniel reassured the flustered woman. 'How can I help?'

'This is Fiona Tarbuck. I'm a Staff Nurse in Cardiac ICU and I'm trying to track down one of the nurses from your unit—Jenny Barber. You wouldn't happen to know where she is, would you? We've tried her landline in her flat and her mobile but there's no answer on either phone. Either she's switched them off, or else her battery's…'

Daniel's attention had been caught by the woman's introduction.

'CICU?' he questioned, interrupting her rambling speculations.

'Yes, that's right. Unfortunately, her father was brought in during the night and her mother's been trying to contact her to let her know. Apparently, their daughter's not on duty, today, but one of your staff suggested she might have told you what she was going to be doing on her day off?'

'No, she didn't say, but—'

'In that case, I'm very sorry to have disturbed you,' she interrupted before he could find the words he needed. How could he say he'd pass the message on without ruining Jenny's reputation for ever by revealing that she was here in his arms?

When the voice was swiftly replaced in his ear by the buzz of a finished call he was left with the task of finding a new set of words—the ones that would break the news that her father was in CICU.

'Daniel?' A concerned frown had appeared, deep enough to pleat the smooth skin of her forehead as she'd tried to follow his cryptic questions and answers. 'You said CICU. That wasn't about Aliyah's husband, was it? Please tell me he hasn't taken a turn for the worse,' she begged, her empathy for their patient completely transparent.

He hated the fact that the news he had to break would cause this caring woman even greater stress, but he had no option. If her father's condition was serious—and the very fact that he was in CICU was proof that it very well could be—then every moment's delay could jeopardise her chance of reaching his bedside in time.

'I'm sorry, Jenny,' he began, desperately fighting the urge to wrap her tightly in his arms in an attempt to soften the blow. 'That was CICU—as you probably gathered. They've been trying to reach you to—'

'*Me?*' she echoed, clearly startled, then panic flared in her eyes. 'Who…? What…? Not *Dad*?' she gasped in sudden comprehension, her body totally rigid against him.

'Unfortunately, yes,' he confirmed. 'He was taken ill during the night.'

'What happened?' she demanded, suddenly frantically fighting her way out from under the cosy nest of bed-clothes, still apparently uncaring of the fact that she was utterly, tantalisingly naked.

'I've no idea of the specifics,' he admitted, battling the urge to gaze his fill of her beautiful body in case it was the last time he ever got to see it—all those lean, slender curves that set his pulse throbbing anew with the urgent need to trace them and savour them and… 'The Staff Nurse didn't go into it,' he admitted as he forced himself to drag his eyes away, turning to reach for clean underwear in the top drawer beside the bed. 'All I know is that they haven't been able to reach you on your landline or your mobile and wondered if I had any idea what you were planning to do today.'

He was already slipping his feet into his shoes while he thrust his arms into a clean shirt, having long ago perfected the knack of speedy dressing. When he turned back to her, Jenny was still trying to find the last of the clothing he'd tossed aside so cavalierly in his urgent need to have her in his arms and in his bed.

'And I was here, with a flat battery in my mobile,' she wailed, self-recrimination obvious in her voice. 'Oh, Daniel…!'

'Hey, Jennywren!' he soothed, discovering her second shoe buried under the pillow that had been tossed to the floor some time after midnight and handed it to her. 'She didn't say the situation's urgent, so don't automatically assume the worst.'

'But she was ringing round trying to find me…she rang my *boss*, for heaven's sake!' she exclaimed. 'That hardly sounds like *"Oh, it's all right, Mr Barber, patients confuse indigestion for heart attacks all the time"*, does it?'

'It doesn't sound like *"It's time to organise the funeral"*, either,' he pointed out sharply, walking the tightrope between sympathy and helping her to keep herself together. 'If you're ready, let's go.'

'Go?' There was a wildly unfocused look in her eyes as she gazed around his little hallway as though she couldn't really work out what she needed to do next.

'I'll drive you to the hospital,' he said, holding up his keys.

'Oh, you don't need to do that. I can take a taxi,' she said immediately, but he was already shaking his head.

'You could, but do you really want to make a phone call to order one, then stand here waiting for it to arrive? It'll be quicker if I take you and drop you off at the closest entrance to CICU.'

He was relieved when she acquiesced, hating the thought that she might have preferred to get herself to the hospital; hating even more the thought that she might not have wanted to have him with her, especially after what had happened between them last night.

Somehow, the attraction he'd felt towards her right from the first day he'd met her—the impossible attraction he'd tried so hard to subdue under the twin guises of professionalism and friendship—had not only exploded into passion, but that passion had given birth to a deeper emotion… a feeling of *connection* that he'd never felt before, with anyone.

* * *

'Thank you so much, Daniel,' Jenny managed in spite of the fact that her thoughts were so impossibly scattered that manners were absolutely the last thing on her mind.

'You're welcome, Jenny,' he said, and his hand came out to trap the one she'd left hanging in mid-air, uncertain whether what had happened between them the night before gave her the right to curl her fingers around the back of his head and pull him close enough for a kiss, the way she wanted to. Blandly shaking his hand certainly didn't feel right...but then, she doubted whether any sort of contact between them would ever feel bland again.

'Let me know how your father's getting on,' he continued, his expression apparently every bit as calmly caring as it always was when he added, 'or if there's anything I can do for you.'

You could come up to be with me while I find out whether Dad's going to be all right, she thought, knowing she definitely didn't have the right to ask that of him. But the thought of having Daniel at her side, of having his hand to hold on to while she learned the worst...

'Thank you,' she said again, knowing that this was something she was going to have to face by herself. Then, when she would have climbed out of the car he suddenly reached out again to put a hand on her arm.

'I mean it, Jenny,' he said, the unexpectedly intent expression in his eyes stopping her breath in her throat for several seconds. 'If you don't call me, I'll come up to look for you...to find out what's going on.'

'Okay,' Jenny agreed breathlessly, suddenly warmed by his evident sincerity even as her heart kicked out an extra couple of beats when she remembered just how potent those eyes could be when they were focused on her. 'I promise I'll let you know as soon as there's anything to tell you.'

'And just for the record,' he added even as she had the door open and one foot on the ground, 'I might seem cool, calm and unaffected by the tragedies we sometimes see, but *seem* is the operative word.'

It was several hours before she had the chance to tell Daniel that her father had undergone balloon angioplasty... at his own insistence. In spite of the advice of the cardiac consultant and the urging of his wife and daughter, he had completely refused to agree to bypass surgery on the grounds that he couldn't afford to take that much time away from work.

Jenny had serious doubts that the procedure would be a long-term success at restoring adequate circulation through her father's heart. The wretched man was so firmly set in his ways that his terrible diet and dire lack of exercise would only cause the whole situation to recur. As heartless as it might seem to anyone else, she had the feeling that only the enforced absence from work that major surgery would entail would give the man the incentive to take a long hard look at what his lifestyle was doing to him.

At least, that was the conclusion she'd reached as she'd sat in the relatives' waiting room, ostensibly to keep her mother company—although what company the workaholic woman needed when she'd spent a good part of her time on the telephone while her husband was undergoing the procedure, Jenny wasn't sure.

Forty-eight hours later, the situation hadn't changed much and Jenny was almost at her wit's end, especially as her father was insisting on discharging himself and her mother was calmly proposing that, if he needed anyone to watch over him, it would have to be Jenny as her own patients certainly couldn't do without her.

For a moment Jenny was completely speechless at the

arrogance of the assumption that a nurse's worth was so much less to her patients than a doctor's. That was apart from the fact that the man in question might be Jenny's father, but he was Helen Sinclair's husband, and as such, should be *her* primary concern.

Of course, the fact that Jenny had already had to take a leave of absence from her own job for the past couple of days on compassionate grounds, and hadn't had a chance to speak to Daniel beyond leaving updates on his voicemail, had absolutely nothing to do with it.

'No, Mother,' she said firmly, stopping the woman in her tracks when she was already halfway out of the door.

'What?' Helen's brain was obviously already focusing on the place she would rather be…with her patients. 'No… *what*, Jennifer?' She glanced at her watch and made the swift double-click of exasperation with her tongue that had been a constant soundtrack to Jenny's entire childhood. 'I really don't have time for pointless riddles.'

'In that case, let me make myself very clear, Mother,' she said, keeping a pleasant smile on her face in spite of her sad resignation to the fact that the woman was unlikely ever to change. She certainly wouldn't have been expecting outright rebellion from the daughter who sometimes felt as if she had spent her whole life trying to please…and failing. 'I will be returning to work tomorrow morning because my colleagues have been left short-handed by my absence and we have patients who could die if there aren't enough of us there to look after them.'

'But… You…' her mother spluttered, clearly as stunned as if the rather etiolated potted plant in the corner of the room had started speaking to her, but Jenny had no intention of letting her speak before *she'd* finished what she needed to say.

'Apart from that, he's *your* husband, not mine, so it's

only right that he should have *you* at his side while he recovers. I'll visit, of course,' she added swiftly when it looked as if her mother was starting to rally her thoughts to mount a counter-offensive. 'I'll come every day, either as soon as I finish my shift, or in the morning if I'm on a late. You can always send me a text if there's anything you need me to bring.'

She hoped that her mother couldn't tell how badly she was shaking as she bestowed their usual cursory cheek-to-cheek excuse for a kiss before she strode briskly out of the waiting room, taking with her the familiar scent of her elegant parent's signature perfume.

She was still shaking when she reached the familiar surroundings of the unit and tapped in the code to open the security lock.

'Jenny! You look dreadful!' Daniel exclaimed…the very last person she'd wanted to meet until she'd got herself a little better under control but absolutely the first person she would have chosen to pour out her latest troubles. 'Is your father worse?' he demanded as he took her elbow and led her into his office. 'I thought he was on the mend.'

'He is…sort of,' she agreed, her concentration scrambled by the solicitous arm he'd wrapped around her shoulders. 'Everyone knows that the angioplasty is only ever going to be a short-term fix for the problem and now he's insisting on signing himself out first thing tomorrow morning… AMA, of course.'

'And you're worried that he's not going to be able to help throwing himself back into the thick of things before he's properly recovered?'

'That goes without saying,' she said wryly. 'There are always more patients waiting to see him, but at least he can't start operating before he's been signed off as fit. That doesn't mean that he won't push himself to do everything else, though.'

'But that's not why you're upset, now,' he said after the briefest of pauses, and the fact that he'd made it a statement of fact rather than a question left her uncomfortably aware that he was the first person who'd ever been able to read her so accurately. 'Did you have an argument with him about going home too soon?'

She shook her head. 'Not with him. There'd be no point,' she said with a resigned shrug. 'He's always been a law unto himself. Even his surgeon admitted it when he couldn't persuade him to have the bypass surgery he should have had…or at least to have stents put in to hold the arteries open far enough to allow some sort of normal circulation.'

'So, what did happen?' He'd perched on the front corner of his desk with one foot propped on the edge of the chair beside hers so that he was distractingly within touching distance. At least his proximity had provided enough of a diversion to stop her shaking.

'I told my mother, categorically, that I would *not* be extending my leave of absence to take care of Dad when he goes home…that he was *her* husband and *she* should be the one to spend that time with him.'

'And she thought you should be the one to stay with him because…?' He did that raised-eyebrow trick that always fascinated her when he used it to signify that he was waiting for her to fill in the blanks.

'Because *I'm* only a nurse while *she's* a doctor and therefore her work is *so* much more important than mine,' she finished for him, clenching her hands into fists when the angry tremble came back into them.

'If you're talking about balancing life-saving surgery against emptying a bedpan, then she would have a point,' he said, then put up a staying hand so that she wouldn't interrupt before he'd finished. 'But if you're balancing an hour or two's attention in an operating theatre with an unconscious patient against days—possibly weeks—of the sort of minute-by-minute, face-to-face, meticulous nursing that can be required to return that patient to good health, then the scales would come down heavily on *that* side of the fence, every time.'

'But just because *you* understand that, it doesn't stop me feeling sick that my parents will never be able to accept my choice of profession; that I'll never be the daughter they hoped for.'

'I take it you're an only child,' he commented, 'or she'd have a second choice of babysitter for your father.'

Diverted by the personal remark she gave him a thoughtful look. 'Whereas you are either the youngest of two or an only, like me,' she decided.

'What makes you say that?' There was a quizzical smile hovering while he waited for her explanation.

'Well, most "onlys" I've known…provided they haven't been spoiled rotten by their parents…have been driven to succeed, and the fact that you reached consultant as early as you did would bear that out.'

'And second children?' he prompted.

'All the ones I've met have been either fiercely resentful of their older siblings or fiercely competitive.' She paused, waiting for a reply, then prompted impatiently, 'Well, which is it? If I were a betting person I'd say you were an only child.'

'Spot on, but in my case it was also single parent as my sperm donor decamped as soon as he learned I was on the way.'

She blinked, surprised that he'd volunteered quite so much and even more surprised by the feeling of connection that knowledge brought with it when she'd only seized on the topic to keep his attention away from her previous lack of control.

She'd had absolutely no idea that she was going to give vent to all those feelings that had been boiling inside her for almost as long as she could remember. It wasn't like her. Usually, she was far too aware of her parents' standing in the hospital to be so indiscreet, but there was just something about Daniel Carterton—about the way he seemed to value her as a colleague—that had made her drop her defences, but had she dropped them a little too far?

In spite of the new feeling of connection that the revelation of their matching only-child status seemed to have formed, she would have to watch out for that and guard against doing it again.

That was especially important in view of his response to the night they'd spent together. Much to her disappointment, instead of taking their tentative friendship to a new level of intimacy, he seemed to have completely backed off from any sort of personal contact with her. In fact this was the first time she'd seen him since he'd dropped her off at the hospital the morning her father had been admitted.

'So much for being guided by your instincts,' she muttered under her breath, later, as she double-checked the equipment trolley, case notes and test results ready for the clinic that afternoon, wondering how she could have got it so wrong. She certainly hadn't taken Daniel for being in the same league as Colin, only interested in her company for what he could get out of it.

In Colin's case, it was blatantly obvious that he saw her as the fast track to a giant leap in his career. In Daniel's…what? Had she been nothing more than a one-night stand when they both needed consolation after a horrendous day?

'Live and learn, Jenny,' she murmured softly, determinedly ignoring the ache around her heart. 'Live and learn.'

Except she had a horrible feeling that it was going to be harder than that to do it. Idiot that she was, she'd probably fallen for Daniel the first time she'd met him; the first time she'd seen the way his smile had lit up those beautiful sapphire eyes.

Then, of course, there was the small fact that, in spite of the overwhelming emotional tension of that day, she would never have made love with him *without* loving him. But that was *her* problem, not his, as was the fact that she couldn't see that situation changing. With her luck, she would probably still be hopelessly in love with him when she was a creaky-limbed eighty-year-old.

So, it all came down to looking at the situation logically, not emotionally, she told herself firmly. For now, they had to work together and she would have to make certain he never guessed how she felt, because that would just be too awkward to bear on a daily basis and she really didn't want to have to leave, not when it was obvious that working with him was all she could ever have of him.

Anyway, there wasn't much she could do about the situation if he was happy with things the way they were between them.

CHAPTER FOUR

DANIEL wasn't happy.

It had been nearly a month since the night he and Jenny had…since her father's collapse, he continued inside his head, not even allowing himself to *think* about what else had happened that night.

And that was part of his problem. The fact that he refused to think about it didn't mean that the events of that night weren't stored in exquisite detail in his brain, just waiting to be resurrected on a nightly basis as soon as his head hit the pillow.

It was slowly driving him crazy.

Or, maybe not so slowly, he thought when he saw her coming out of the staffroom with a worried expression on her face and immediately felt the need to find out what was wrong. Perhaps he'd already gone right around the bend when his concern for one particular member of staff could push everything else completely out of his head.

There were so many unassailable reasons why there should be nothing more than a professional relationship between the two of them, the fact that she was a junior member of staff in the same department being just the least of them, but he was definitely going to go demented if he couldn't talk to her—to have at least one conversation to try to clear the air between them. After all, trying to ignore the fact that the two of them had spent the night together wasn't going to help the memory fade from his mind any time soon, and he needed his brain back in working order *before* he made a serious clinical error.

'Jenny, do you think you could—?' he began.

'Daniel, I need to talk to you—' she started simultaneously.

'After you—' he said, utterly relieved that he wasn't going to have to find the words to ask her if she would go out for a drink with him. He was uncomfortably aware that it felt horribly like the first time he'd ever tried to ask a girl out…and got shot down in flames for his trouble.

'No, after you,' she demurred after a silence that seemed to stretch out into infinity, then leapt into the void, anyway. 'I was just hoping you would have a few minutes free after work this evening, that we could have a coffee, or something, and talk.'

Finally, she ran out of words, like a child's toy that needed winding up before it could chatter its way around the floor again.

'Of course.' Was it really going to be this easy? 'What time were you thinking? Sevenish?'

She pulled a wry face, wordlessly acknowledging the fact that shifts in a hospital rarely ended on time. 'Sevenish,' she agreed, her expression gratifyingly lighter than it had been just a few minutes ago, although there was still an unfamiliar shadow lurking behind those beautiful eyes.

Well, now was not the time to worry about it. There was obviously enough left of their fledgling friendship for her to have felt she could come to him when she needed a sounding board for whatever was on her mind. And if she had secrets and had chosen him to confide in, well, he couldn't help but be aware of the little bubble of hope that started to swell inside him, or stop himself from glancing at the clock to see just how many minutes there were until he'd be seeing her again.

'Can I get you something to drink, Jenny?' he offered, his wallet already in his hand as they reached the softly lit bar. 'White wine, or something stronger?'

She shook her head and hoped her smile didn't look as shaky as it felt.

'An orange juice, please, topped up with lemonade… I'm always desperate for fluids when I come off a shift. I suppose it's a combination of spending so many hours in such a warm environment and not taking in enough liquids during the day—not having enough time to drink at all, most of the time—a common complaint among doctors and nurses. And if the liquids you *do* drink are coffee, which acts as a diuretic…'

She closed her eyes as soon as he turned away to place their orders, mortified that she was doing that nervous-chattering thing again but totally unable to bear any silence between them, afraid that she might say too much, too soon.

Thank goodness, for the sake of her sanity, Daniel took over the conversation at that point, telling her how he'd come across this little out-of-the-way pub almost a year ago on a similarly bitterly cold night.

'This little valley seems to catch the worst of the weather every winter and the frost was so hard that it almost looked as if there'd been a light fall of snow. The roads were getting treacherously slick and I'd just decided to look for somewhere safe to turn around when I saw the lights of this place up ahead and couldn't resist,' he related as they navigated a route through the scattering of wooden tables with drinks in hand and found a quiet table in the bay of one of the front windows.

The cosy room wasn't big enough for any true seclusion, but there was just enough chatter from the other patrons and the group bantering with the landlord at one end of the bar that it was doubtful that anyone would overhear their conversation.

Still, the subject she wanted to bring up meant that relaxing was impossible, and Daniel didn't look as if he was sure how to begin now that he'd exhausted the topic of how he'd initially found the place.

Her heart sank as she realised just how little likelihood there was that this evening would end well. She'd known before she'd even approached him earlier today that it was highly unlikely that they would ever be on their old friendly footing again, but...

'I hope you don't mind, but I ordered two plates of lasagne, as well. It's home-made and rather good,' he added hurriedly, a look of apology on his face when she just sat staring at him, wondering when he'd managed to organise that without her hearing a word of it.

'Jenny?' he prompted gently and reached out to touch the clenched fists resting in her lap. 'One thing at a time, one decision at a time. First decision, would you like lasagne or no lasagne?'

She had to blink hard against the sudden hot press of tears brought on by his typically Daniel consideration, but she managed to find a glimpse of the smile he deserved. 'Lasagne, please,' she confirmed. 'I'm starving.'

'So, how's your father doing?' he asked and she almost leapt on the new topic with relief, glad that she was able to make him laugh as she told of her mother's exasperation with a husband she swore was as recalcitrant as a two-year-old.

The meal was every bit as good as he'd said it would be. Unfortunately, the last few mouthfuls were spoiled by the knowledge that the time for one of the most important conversations of her life was approaching with the speed of an express train; the knowledge that her relationship with the man who had been slowly winding himself around her heart from the first time she'd met him would never be the same after she told him—

'Oh!' She felt herself shriek as something crashed into her side, sending her flying, and the peaceful atmosphere around them was shattered by the most unbelievably loud mixture of noises. Sounds that convinced Jenny that a bomb had been detonated in the room as glass and furniture thudded and crashed around her.

Just seconds later all was relatively silent for the space of a single breath, then the screams and moans of the wounded rose up all around them, almost hiding the sound of running feet somewhere outside the enormous hole now letting the icy air blow across her.

'Jenny? Are you all right?' Daniel demanded urgently from the other side of their upturned table. 'I'm ringing for the emergency services but we'll need to start some sort of triage.'

'I'm okay,' she told him, wincing as she tried to wriggle out from under the surprisingly heavy table without Daniel knowing. There could be far worse injuries to deal with around them than the few bruises she would have to show. 'Can you find out what happened so we have some idea what we'll be dealing with? Was it a gas explosion in the kitchen, or what?'

She heard his feet crunching over broken glass somewhere nearby, but with the sudden darkness pressing down on her she was barely able to stop herself from begging him not to leave her. And how stupid was that when she was perfectly able to extricate herself and do something to help others unable to help themselves?

'It was a car,' he announced, appearing just as she'd managed to struggle to her feet, looming through the thick pall of dust hanging in the air. 'It must have been travelling too fast when it hit a patch of black ice on the hill outside this place and couldn't stop. We're lucky it only hit the wall before it stopped or we could have had a car parked inside the pub.'

'Is anyone trapped in it?' she demanded as she shook her head gingerly, grimacing at the sound of the falling shards of glass.

'No. I heard whoever was in it legging it, so either they'd stolen the car or they were driving under the influence and didn't want to be breathalysed.'

'I hope they weren't hurt,' she murmured as they moved in tandem through the dimly lit room, grateful for the candles the publican was lighting as they righted chairs and tables in their path, checking each place where, such a short time ago, people had been enjoying a peaceful evening. 'What happened to the lights?'

'Obviously the circuit's been damaged somewhere and tripped the fuses. The publican said it's probably safer to leave it off till it's been checked,' he explained. 'Give me a shout if you need any help.'

Jenny was grateful for the pub's plentiful supply of water and paper serviettes as she came across several patrons who had been wounded by flying glass over the next few minutes. It took longer to reassure them that help was on its way than it did to provide makeshift dressings for those that needed covering.

She suspected that the older lady who'd put out a hand to save herself when she'd tripped in the dark had probably broken her wrist, but that was the most severe injury she encountered, and the landlord's first-aid supplies provided the sling she needed to make the stalwart lady comfortable enough to await transport to hospital.

She'd been so busy going from person to person, certain that there must have been some more serious injuries from such a catastrophic accident, that she'd all but forgotten her own injuries. It wasn't until Daniel called and she twisted to check on his whereabouts that the pain in her ribs grabbed her with vicious claws and she nearly passed out.

Lightning flashes filled her vision and she was totally unable to draw breath for several endless seconds before she was able to loosen her desperate grip on the back of a nearby chair, suddenly realising with a sinking feeling that she might have been a little more severely injured than she'd initially thought.

'Fire and Rescue,' said a voice from somewhere out in the cold darkness.

'Thank God,' Jenny said, glad that their ordeal was nearly over, even as she wondered when she would have a chance to go back to the conversation they should have been having by now. Part of her was relieved that the fateful moment had been delayed, but the greater part wished that it was already over; that she knew what his reaction had been when she'd told him—

'Are you injured, Miss?' called a voice somewhere behind her and she gingerly turned just far enough to see the paramedic's uniform.

'I'm fine,' she tried to reassure him, squinting against the bright torch he was aiming in her direction.

'Are you sure?' he challenged and she had to give him points for his powers of observation. 'You look as if you've got a very sparkly case of dandruff, there. Rather a lot of glass obviously landed on you.'

'I can shake it off when I get outside,' she said dismissively then gestured in the direction of the elderly lady she'd just been tending. 'Gladys, here, is your next patient. Query Colles' fracture, left arm.'

When the time came for her patient to be loaded into the ambulance, she suddenly became very tearful and begged Jenny to come with her.

She was torn, one part of her only too willing to give the shaken woman the reassurance of a familiar face while the other wished that there was enough time to speak to Daniel, to say something before she went, to tell him... what?

Tell him that she was sorry that she'd made a mess of things by falling apart on him that night. Tell him that she missed his smiles, his jokes, the way his eyes used to sparkle at her when they were sharing a moment of triumph when a woman who had tried to start a family for years without success was finally able to hold her precious baby. Tell him that she missed spending time with him, even if it was only for a cup of coffee at the end of a long shift. Tell him that she loved—

'Go with your patient,' Daniel said easily, giving her hand a little squeeze that shouldn't have had any effect on her pulse. 'Get yourself checked over at the same time. I'll catch up with you in A and E,' and the decision was made.

Mounting the steps into the back of the ambulance without revealing her discomfort hadn't been easy, but the sharp shards of agony that any movement sent through her ribs was marginally relieved by wrapping her arms around herself.

Still, at least Daniel wasn't there to see that she was in pain. The last thing she wanted was for him to treat her as an injured patient. For her own peace of mind, it was important for the sake of any future relationship between the two of them that he should see her as a competent professional colleague.

'Here,' said the paramedic as he grabbed a thick cellular blanket from a nearby locker and wrapped its soft warmth around her.

'How is she doing?' she asked with a nod towards the older woman, noting that she looked rather wan.

'Not very comfortable, but definitely happier now you're with her,' he reported cheerfully.

Well, at least that was something, Jenny consoled herself while she tried to brace herself against the movement of the ambulance without giving any hint of her growing discomfort.

She'd heard that broken ribs were inordinately painful, but she was desperately hoping that wasn't what was causing the agony every time she moved. She really didn't want to be forced to take time off work so she was hoping that she'd be able to convince anyone who asked that she'd suffered nothing more serious than bruising.

As for her hip, at her age it was highly unlikely that she would have broken it in a mere fall, so it was just a case of putting up with the ache until the discomfort of the bruising resolved itself.

'You'll have to get out first, so we've got room to manoeuvre,' the paramedic announced as the ambulance braked before reversing into position in front of the emergency entrance. 'As you're staff, you'll be allowed to follow us through.'

The double doors swung wide and Jenny gingerly stepped out first as the paramedic helped Gladys out of the ambulance and into the waiting wheelchair. Then she was hobbling in its wake, glad that Daniel wasn't there to catch sight of her struggles.

With Gladys whisked out of sight, no doubt destined for

X-rays and the plaster room, Jenny made her way towards the A and E waiting area feeling decidedly at a loose end until Daniel arrived.

Tentatively, she lowered herself into one of the ubiquitous plastic chairs, barely suppressing a grimace as her painful hip came into contact with the unforgiving surface.

'So, you didn't escape without a bump or two, did you?' said a man's voice and she looked up in surprise to see several of the people to whom she'd given assistance back in the dusty nightmare of the damaged pub.

'Just a couple of bruises,' she said dismissively. 'How are you doing?'

'Not so bad,' said his wife with a smile. 'The nurse said they'd get to us as soon as possible—that we're both going to need a couple of stitches when they've checked that there isn't any glass left in the cuts—but we know we're not emergencies and there are people who need help before we do.' Suddenly, a thought struck her. 'My dear, you wouldn't know what happened to the people in the car, would you? Were they very badly hurt?'

'We don't know whether they were hurt because they ran away from the scene,' she said.

'Ran away?' the woman said in amazement. 'Why on earth would anyone…?'

'Joyriders!' her husband interrupted in disgusted tones. 'Although why it should be called that, I'll never know because it certainly doesn't seem to bring much joy…to the car's owner, the police, even to the stupid kids if they injure themselves driving too fast, to say nothing of the other people they injure. The government should bring back conscription. That would teach them some discipline and a sense of responsibility.'

'Don't you start, John,' his wife scolded in what was obviously a well-worn argument, and Jenny was able to tune them out, wondering if she shouldn't just take herself home rather than wait for Daniel. All she really needed was to hang her head over a large sheet of newspaper with a brush to get rid of the glass, and as for her ribs and her hip, nothing but time was needed to cure her bruises.

If that was all true, why was she still sitting there with her eyes flicking constantly towards the door, waiting for Daniel to appear?

Admit it, she berated herself silently. *You're just looking for an excuse to spend more time with the man.*

She could hardly argue with that thought, because it was true. In the last month, she'd missed those precious off-duty moments they'd spent together and had been storing up the unexpected bonus of eating a meal together this evening before she had to broach the conversation that could put a permanent barrier between them.

She shifted uncomfortably in her seat, again, and this time it was her ribs that caused her to draw in a sharp hiss of breath.

'Jenny?' said a voice beside her as her elderly companions chimed in.

'There you are, young man! How is everyone? Did that poor woman break her arm?'

'She's in good hands, now,' Daniel reassured them without breaching patient confidentiality, just as she had.

'That's good to hear. Very good to hear. Now, have you come to look after this young lady?'

'This one?' Daniel asked with a frown as he finally met her gaze.

'Yes. That one,' the elderly man said firmly. 'She spent all that time taking care of everyone else, and all the while she was injured, herself.'

'Injured?' She saw Daniel's eyes darken with concern

as he reached out a hand to lift dusty wisps of hair off her forehead. 'Where are you injured, Jenny?'

'It's nothing,' she tried to reassure him, but she might as well have saved herself the effort; he obviously wasn't buying it.

'Come with me,' he said, holding out a rather scratched hand to her. 'I'll get someone in Triage to check you over.'

'It's really not necessary,' she began but it didn't look as if he was taking no for an answer when he wrapped those long fingers around her wrist and tugged, making both her hip and her ribs stab her simultaneously.

'No arguments,' he decreed as he led her across the room towards the central desk. 'Is there anyone free to check this stubborn woman over?' he demanded. 'She's one of the victims from the pub crash and hasn't been seen by anyone, yet.'

She was going to point out that she was perfectly capable of asking for help if she wanted it, but when Daniel turned towards her she caught a brief glimpse of something that looked like abject guilt and, much though she didn't want to have her personal diagnosis of cracked ribs confirmed, couldn't deprive him of the peace of mind that allowing herself to be examined would give him.

In a very few minutes she was in a cubicle behind a drawn curtain and had finally had to admit that she might need some help when she couldn't pull her jumper over her head to get the voluminous cotton gown on.

'Dammit, Jennywren, why didn't you tell me you'd been hurt, too?' Daniel growled when he stepped behind her to tie the inevitable gown and caught sight of her bruises for the first time.

He felt sick when he saw the livid purple welt across

her ribs, and so guilty that he hadn't even suspected that she might be in pain.

'How did this happen? Why didn't you say something?'

'For the simple reason that it wasn't important when there were patients to triage,' she declared. 'It's only a couple of bruises caused by the edge of the table and when I fell on the floor, neither of which were your fault, so take that guilty expression off your face.'

'Fine!' he exclaimed, and found himself flinging both hands up in the air in a most unlikely gesture of surrender. 'We'll agree not to argue, then. I'll agree not to argue about who's responsible for your injuries if you'll agree not to argue about having X-rays to check that nothing's broken. Deal?'

If anything, her face went even paler, especially when she shook her head and had to grab for her painful ribs.

'*No* deal,' she said, her strained voice only serving to make him more determined to get those pictures. 'The National Radiological Protection Board frowns on the taking of unnecessary X-rays.'

Daniel gritted his teeth at her obstinacy and wished heartily that they were having this discussion somewhere rather more private than a curtained cubicle surrounded by dozens of other people, both patients and staff.

He doubted she'd punctured a lung—her symptoms were obviously uncomfortable but weren't severe enough for that—but there was definitely something more than a couple of bruises going on, colourful though they may be, and he was determined to find out what. He was sure there must be something that needed attention, or Jenny wouldn't be standing there with a chalk-white face clutching her ribs and avoiding putting her weight on one hip. He didn't need to be an A and E consultant to make that diagnosis.

'On the other hand,' he argued, 'the GMC would frown heavily if a doctor were negligent in the care of a patient, for example, in not taking X-rays when their use was clinically indicated.'

'Except if the patient were to exercise his or her right to refuse treatment,' she countered stubbornly. 'And anyway, I'm not your patient.'

'Dammit, Jenny, what is wrong with you?' he growled, hanging on to his temper by a fraying thread as he positioned the purloined wheelchair beside her, ready to push her wherever she needed to go. And all the while the thought that he'd blithely directed her to help everybody else when she was injured herself—injured and had never so much as hinted that she was in pain as she'd spent time examining people and reassuring them—had his guilt ballooning.

'It's only an X-ray, for heaven's sake!' he exclaimed as she folded her arms around her ribs, evidently refusing to budge in spite of the fact she could be risking a punctured lung. 'You know as well as I do that it will only take a couple of seconds to be certain you don't have any serious injuries, and it won't hurt a bit.'

'Won't hurt *me*, you mean,' she whispered through trembling lips, her hazel eyes wide and fearful as she focused them on him.

For several heartbeats he stood there as the overwhelming significance of that tiny sentence detonated inside his brain, his gaze trapped by the mixture of emotions in her expression.

Helplessly, he found himself staring at the slender body lost in voluminous patterned cotton, even though he knew it was far too soon for there to be any evidence of the miracle going on inside her.

'Jennifer?' called a commanding voice as the curtain

behind him was drawn swiftly aside. 'Have you been for an X-ray, yet? Have you broken anything?' demanded her father, flanked by not only his wife but the smugly loathsome Fletcher, too, and when he saw the gaggle of interested bystanders clogging up the corridor, Daniel knew that this definitely wasn't the place where this conversation should be taking place.

CHAPTER FIVE

'WHAT'S going on? *Has* she had any X-rays yet?' her father demanded again almost before the door of the interview room had closed behind them, as usual hating not to be in charge of whatever was going on.

It hadn't taken Daniel long to whisk them along the corridor to the relatives' interview room and Jenny could almost have thrown her arms around him in gratitude for his consideration. There must have been almost a dozen people within sight of that curtained cubicle, and heaven only knew how many more within earshot.

'Jenny won't be having any X-rays,' Daniel said as he stood beside her, one reassuring hand warm on her shoulder, and for the first time Jenny knew the delightful feeling of knowing that she wasn't going to be facing her parents alone. 'It's not considered advisable in the early stages of a pregnancy.'

'You're *pregnant*?'

The words were spoken almost in unison in equal tones of incredulity by the three people facing them and Jenny didn't think she'd ever been so embarrassed before, but it wasn't the embarrassment that would remain in her memory for ever so much as the different expressions on her audience's faces.

Her parents wore almost identical masks of disapproval

and disappointment...but when had they ever looked at her in any other way?

After his initial blank-faced shock, Colin's expression had become a strange mixture of calculation and determination as he worked out how to turn this unexpected situation to his advantage. She could easily imagine him rubbing his hands with the gleeful thought that her father's shoes were about to be handed to him on the same platter that would hold her head.

She couldn't even bring herself to meet Daniel's eyes, knowing just how much he must hate being mixed up in such an unsavoury situation, and her heart felt like a lump of lead in her chest at the opportunity she'd missed to tell him her news in a less public way; to explain that, despite the fact her stupidity had forced him into the position of becoming a father, she had absolutely no intention of trying to use the pregnancy to tie him to her...much as she might want to.

'Oh, but this is *wonderful* news, darling,' Colin burbled with a smile as wide as a letterbox showing every one of his thirty-two chemically whitened teeth. 'Now you'll have to get busy organising the wedding, won't you?' he added gleefully as he walked towards her with his arms spread wide, only to have Daniel step in his path with a determined expression on his face.

'Just a moment, Fletcher,' he said in growling tones reminiscent of a very big, very powerful guard dog with a trespasser in his sights. 'I wouldn't go counting your chickens *just* yet.'

'This is hardly any of *your* business,' the shorter man sneered smugly. 'You might be Jennifer's boss, but her parents already know that I've proposed to her. All this does is brings the date forward a bit.'

'Hardly!' Daniel snorted dismissively. 'I know for a

fact that Jenny has refused your proposal, in no uncertain terms, so I think it's highly unlikely that she'll be hurrying to organise a wedding with you under *any* circumstances, and certainly not these.'

The whole situation was already making her feel distinctly uncomfortable, and the only redeeming factor she could think of was that neither Clive nor her parents knew about the night she'd spent with Daniel. In her parents' eyes, the very fact that she was pregnant without being married was tantamount to a declaration that she was totally without morals.

She was overwhelmingly grateful that Daniel had transferred the whole conversation behind closed doors. The last thing she needed was for this information to be broadcast right around the hospital. Her parents would never forgive her for bringing such shame on the family.

The fact that she was now shut in a room with both of her parents and with Colin doing his best to ingratiate himself with her father made her feel even more queasy, but there was no way out of it. The least she could do was face them on her feet rather than having them all talking down at her, but that was easier said than done when everything was hurting so much.

Then Daniel's arm wrapped gently around her shoulders to support her as she pushed her way out of the chair, and when he automatically made certain that the fabric of the flimsy hospital gown was wrapped firmly across her back to preserve her modesty, she suddenly felt the warmth of certainty that there was at least one person in the room who would stand up for her in the coming argument.

Not that her father was happy about his presence.

'Does *he* have to be here while the family's dirty linen is aired?' her father challenged her with a glare at Daniel.

Jenny had to turn her whole body so that she could

see Daniel's face, causing his arm to slip away from her shoulders. Immediately she felt its loss, but when his lean-fingered hand sought hers among the limp folds of her hospital-issue gown in a wordless gesture of support, she gratefully allowed him to wrap her own in it. The tingling warmth that permeated her whole body made it easy to ignore the glares aimed at them by both her father and Colin.

'*I* want Daniel to be here with me. He's become a good friend,' she said, and as the unexpected words emerged, she suddenly realised that she couldn't have meant them more, in spite of the fact that the two of them had hardly spoken since that fateful night.

'Is it true, Jennifer?' Now it was her mother's turn to take the floor. Her parents had always made concerted attacks when they felt that their daughter wasn't living up to their expectations. '*Are* you pregnant?'

There wasn't a hint of anything other than censure in her sharp tone or her expression; certainly no dawning joy at the realisation that her first grandchild might be on the way.

Still, why should she have expected anything different? It was hard to recall anything she'd done that her mother had approved of, right from her earliest memories of the scoldings she'd received for spoiling the pretty dresses she'd been forced to wear when she'd rather have worn something more suitable for climbing trees and riding bicycles.

Then Daniel's hand tightened just a little bit around hers, his thumb stroking across her knuckles reminding her that she wasn't standing alone, this time…but it also reminded her that she wasn't that little girl any more. She was an adult and it was up to her to deal with her own life's choices.

'Yes, Mother, I'm pregnant,' she agreed with a show of calmness that she definitely wasn't feeling. 'I did a test this morning.'

'Stupid girl!' the elegant older woman hissed, her perfectly unlined complexion a testament to her husband's skill with a knife. 'When have you *ever* managed to do anything right? I suppose it's up to your father and I to sort out yet another mess for you. There isn't time to organise a proper wedding so it'll have to be in the nearest Registry Office.'

'*No*, Mother!' Jenny exclaimed, but she might as well have tried to stop a Centurion tank with a feather duster.

'Colin, can I leave it up to you to find out the earliest possible appointment?' her mother continued, completely ignoring her. 'Jennifer will have to go with you to fill out the forms and I think you'll both need to take your birth certificates with you, but that shouldn't be any…'

'Mrs Sinclair, if I might interrupt for a moment?' Daniel said in a strangely soft tone that sent prickles over Jenny's skin. She didn't think she'd ever heard him speak like that before and certainly wouldn't want to be on the receiving end of it. She could well understand why even her mother went instantly silent. 'Don't you think that telling Fletcher to organise his marriage to your daughter to legitimise her baby might be a bit premature when you haven't even asked her if the baby is his?'

'Of course it's mine!' Colin blustered, suddenly red-faced at the turn the conversation had taken, but she noticed that he didn't make any attempt to meet her eyes. In fact, now that she looked closer, he was definitely avoiding everyone's gaze in a decidedly shifty way. 'And I had every intention of giving Jenny an engagement ring after the dinner dance,' he added suddenly, with the air of a magician pulling a rabbit out of a hat.

'Ah, yes! The dinner dance!' Daniel exclaimed with that steely edge of menace growing with every quietly spoken word. 'That would be the dinner dance that you forced Jenny to attend with you in spite of the fact that she'd already told you she didn't want to go out with you again, would it? The dinner dance where you deliberately got her drunk to make certain that you would have an excuse to escort her home?'

The stupefied expression on her parents' faces was something she'd never thought to see, but it wasn't nearly as riveting as the sickly pallor that was rapidly appearing on her erstwhile suitor's.

'And if you're now claiming that Jenny's pregnant with your child,' he continued inexorably, 'then I doubt that there would be any court in the country that wouldn't convict you of premeditated rape.'

Such an ugly little word and so full of evil that it made her shudder. And she had Daniel to thank that it hadn't happened. Colin's greed and ambition obviously so far outweighed any concepts of decency and honesty that he would even try to claim responsibility for the pregnancy as a way to force her hand.

As for the baby, her only regret was that it was going to be coming into the world without the benefit of a mother and father in a committed, loving relationship, and she had no one to blame for that other than herself.

'I didn't *rape* her!' Colin exclaimed in a panicky voice, suddenly seeming to notice the gaping black hole that had opened at his feet. 'I only topped her glass up a couple of times.'

'You *deliberately* got her drunk? *Why*, for God's sake?' her father demanded, looking utterly dumbfounded. 'Why on earth would you do such a thing to her? You told me you were in love with Jennifer…that you wanted to marry her.'

Colin had the frantic look of a trapped rat and didn't look as if he dared to open his mouth for fear of making the whole situation worse. In the end it was Daniel who put the whole shameful plan into words

'He's probably not honest enough to admit it, but he's *never* been in love with Jenny. He probably only told you that because he thought you would help him to persuade her to marry him. The only thing he really wants is to be your son-in-law,' he said succinctly and Jenny saw Colin flinch at the brutal way he'd worded it. 'At a guess it was part of his master plan…to become part of your family so that he would be at the head of the queue to step straight into your shoes as soon as you retire. Of course, if that part of his plan didn't work…if he didn't get the job in spite of the fact that he was your son-in-law, I don't doubt that the despicable worm was counting on the long-term benefits of marrying her…that all your family wealth and property would drop straight into his greedy hands when you die.'

'Dear God, Fletcher, are you really that venal? Did you really think you could get my daughter drunk and rape her to get an easy life?' Douglas Sinclair was roaring out the words by the time he got to the end, the veins standing out alarmingly at his temples. 'Get out of here and clear your desk. As of this minute you are no longer employed at this hospital. And don't even *think* about asking me for a refer-ence. Oh, and just in case you think you can claim unfair dismissal and use employment law to screw some money out of the hospital, let me remind you that it would only take one word to the appropriate authorities for you to be struck off for what you've done, and for you to be spending time in prison… In fact that's still a distinct possibility, if my daughter decides to make a formal complaint against you…which I really hope she does!'

The look Colin threw in her direction was a disturbing mixture of terror and hate but she couldn't help herself taking personal satisfaction as she hammered the final nail in the coffin of his dreams.

'By the way, Colin, you should have done your research a bit better before you set your sights on me as the fast track to Easy Street and my parents' estate in the country. Didn't anyone ever mention that I'm only their *adopted* daughter; that I don't carry a single drop of Sinclair blood?'

Colin slunk out of the room like a dog with his tail between his legs and Jenny couldn't find a single scrap of regret for his misery because he'd brought it all on himself.

'So,' her father said, his colour slightly less alarming now that the object of his ire had left the room, 'how do you know so much about what's been going on in our daughter's life, Dr…?'

'Carterton. Daniel Carterton,' he supplied but Jenny wasn't willing to relinquish her hold on the security of his hand just yet, even if he'd wanted to offer to shake her father's hand. 'Jenny and I work together. We've been friends for several months…ever since she moved across from NICU.'

'But that doesn't explain how you could possibly know what Fletcher had planned; that he'd got Jennifer drunk to…to try to force her into marriage,' her mother broke in, her voice clipped and precise and obviously intent on getting answers.

Jenny knew of old just how relentless Helen Sinclair could be in one of her inquisitions and her heart sank that Daniel was about to be grilled just because he was here to give her moral support.

'I knew because…' He paused for a fraction of a second

before continuing. 'Because on the night of the party I happened to be in the right place at the right time to see what was happening,' he explained as simply and easily as if he was discussing the weather, apparently completely unaffected by the two pairs of eyes dissecting him. 'And because Jenny and I are close friends, I know that your daughter is far too choosy to want to go to bed with Fletcher voluntarily,' he added pointedly, but only Jenny knew that there was a hidden implication in his words… that she'd had no such reservations about going to bed with Daniel…had virtually propositioned him, in fact.

'So, has she told you who else could be the father of her baby?' It was her father's turn to take over the questioning. 'Do *you* know if she's been seeing anyone else?'

Jenny was just about to leap into the conversation to tell her parents that it was not appropriate to grill her boss about her social life, shuddering at the very thought of her parents' ire being turned on Daniel when it had been at *her* instigation that the two of them had spent the night together, when he answered.

'I'm afraid that is privileged information, sir,' he said formally but impeccably politely. 'Your daughter will have to be the one to tell you when she's ready. That's her right and I wouldn't presume to take it away from her.'

'But that's completely ridiculous and totally unacceptable!' her mother exploded, almost incandescent with rage. 'She's pregnant! In just a few weeks everyone will be able to *see* that she's pregnant! For the sake of the Sinclair name she should be respectably married before that happens.'

'No matter what anybody else deems *acceptable*, I doubt that Jenny would ever get married before she's good and ready, Mrs Sinclair.' Daniel turned just far enough that he could meet her eyes then deliberately held her gaze as he continued. 'She's an adult, and that means *she* gets to make the choices about her own life, regardless of your name.'

His words were an almost uncanny echo of her own thoughts at the beginning of this whole messy confrontation and she was so very grateful for them that she was close to tears.

'In the meantime, she's had a pretty harrowing evening,' he continued, pressing the hand he'd been holding throughout the whole encounter between both of his and smiling reassuringly. 'She was looking after other people in spite of her own injuries—a real credit to both of you—but she should be going to bed to allow her injuries to heal, as well as for the sake of her baby, so if you don't mind…?' He curved his arm around her shoulders again as he settled her back into the wheelchair then pushed her to the door, and to Jenny's absolute amazement, her parents didn't utter a single word of objection.

She held her breath all along the corridor until they turned the first corner before she spoke, her words trembling with a mixture of tension and relief.

'Oh, Daniel, I wish I'd met you at least twenty years ago. My life would have been so much more pleasant if you'd been there to run interference between me and my parents.'

'Oh, I doubt it, Jenny,' he disagreed with an unexpected edge to his voice. 'I was far more obviously from the wrong side of the tracks, back then.' And he doubted that her parents would have even let him in at the tradesmen's entrance to spend time with her, let alone the front door.

'Crazy man,' she chuckled, suddenly unutterably weary. 'Do you know, I don't think I've even got enough energy to get back into my clothes, let alone to get myself home?'

'Well, my car's not far away, so that's one less thing to worry about,' he pointed out so reassuringly that she was quite happy to leave him to make decisions for her while her brain no longer seemed capable of doing so.

In short order, he grabbed a clean set of scrubs and a passing nurse to help her into them, then brought his car right into the hospital forecourt and guided her gently into the front seat.

Instead of her minuscule home with the innumerable stairs, he took her to his own flat, where he insisted on dosing her with analgesia that was safe in pregnancy and tucking her into his own hastily remade bed.

She lay for several delightful moments luxuriating in the pleasure of being surrounded by the scent of freshly laundered bed linen underlain by hints of Daniel's soap and shampoo retained by the pillows and duvet, drawing in the darker notes that could only come from his own body. It was almost like being surrounded by the man himself... almost, but not quite. The bed definitely seemed far too big for one when the last time she'd been in it she'd been sharing it with its owner.

With her brain growing fuzzy with the combination of tiredness, adrenaline let-down and analgesia, it wasn't long before she drifted away into sleep, surfacing briefly when Daniel roused her to swallow the next set of tablets then settling gratefully back onto the pillow and wondering groggily why it felt so much as if it was Daniel's shoulder under her cheek and why his bedclothes cradling her felt so much like being surrounded by his arms.

It was a disappointment when her internal alarm clock woke her a few minutes before six to open her eyes and find herself alone in the bed. More than a disappointment when she'd been so convinced that Daniel had been sharing the bed with her.

'But life is full of disappointments,' she murmured philosophically, then yelped when she tried to roll over to get out of bed and was suddenly reminded in the most painful way that there had been a serious reason why she'd ended up at his flat rather than her own.

She raised her head experimentally, wanting to know just how far she could move before the pain in her ribs grew unbearable, and stopped, transfixed by the hollowed evidence that a head had recently been resting on the pillow beside hers.

'So, I *didn't* imagine it!' she whispered in delight, feeling a grin lifting both corners of her mouth at the realisation that she hadn't been dreaming. Daniel *had* been holding her gently, protectively, in his arms; she *had* been sleeping with her head on his shoulder and his arms around her.

She was tempted to bury her nose in that tantalising hollow to draw his unmistakable scent deep inside her when there was a sound at the bedroom door.

'Awake at last, Sleeping Beauty?' Daniel's voice sounded husky, almost as if he was still half asleep, and his eyes were heavy lidded as they travelled over her among the tumbled bedclothes.

'D-Daniel?' Her pulse accelerated to the speed of sound in the fraction of a second it took to realise that there was now a very intent expression in those wide-awake eyes; an expression that made her very aware of the fact that he was standing just feet away from the bed that they might have shared quite innocently last night, but it was the same bed that they'd shared far from innocently a month ago.

'I made you some tea and toast,' he announced, and finally allowed her to drag her gaze away from his to take in the mug and plate he was holding. 'I nearly made you coffee, but then I remembered…' And just like that, reality brought her crashing to the ground with even greater effect than that out-of-control car last night.

'I was going to tell you last night,' she said. 'That was why I wanted to see you, to talk to you. Well, not just to talk…' Oh, she was making such a mess of this.

'Stop stressing about it, Jenny. I had managed to work that much out for myself,' he said calmly as he deposited the gently steaming mug and the plate piled high with perfectly browned toast. And on the edge of the plate were two white tablets just like the ones he'd given her at intervals during the night.

The memory was clearer now, of him supporting her with a naked arm around her shoulders while she'd downed the glass of water he'd supplied to wash the tablets down. In fact, the memory was far too clear if she was going to be able to avoid blushing while she sat up enough to reach the breakfast he'd brought for her while still keeping the covers high enough for modesty.

'I *have* seen it all before,' he reminded her wickedly, making her fumble, and she lost control of both the bed-clothes and her blush.

'Not while you were standing there fully clothed, you haven't,' she snapped crossly, dragging an armful of duvet up to her chin.

'Well, if that's what's upsetting you, it can be easily remedied,' he said as he reached for the hem of his sweat-shirt.

'Don't you dare!' she squeaked, closing her eyes tightly then groaning when she realised what a fool she must look.

'Ah, Jennywren, I'm sorry. I'll stop teasing you… for now. Here…' He picked up the mug and plate that she'd almost forgotten about while she fought back her blushes, and passed them to her. Then, when she would have thought he'd turn and leave the room, she watched wide-eyed as he moved just one pace away to settle himself at the foot of the bed.

'Listen, we need to talk about a few things,' he said, all traces of humour gone.

'Things,' she repeated blankly, suddenly no more ready for this conversation this morning than she'd been last night, in spite of the fact he already knew the worst.

'Unfortunately, after last night, the hospital grapevine is probably already alive with rumours—'

'Thanks to my parents and Colin,' she interrupted grimly, despairing at the thought that her reputation could have been damaged beyond repair by that weasel, and through no fault of her own. Well, that wasn't strictly true if she were being honest because she had willingly made love with Daniel and *that* had resulted in her pregnancy. But after that less than peaceful meeting in A and E, how long would it be before the whole hospital knew that she was pregnant and the speculation grew about the identity of the baby's father?

Colin had been denied the chance to claim her baby as his, but that wouldn't matter to the grapevine.

'Fletcher's involvement certainly won't have helped matters, especially when word gets round that he's been summarily kicked out of his job,' Daniel agreed coolly, echoing her thoughts, but there was a glimpse of something dark and angry behind his apparent lack of emotion that she knew wasn't aimed at her.

'Nor were things helped by my mother's insistence on trying to arrange the details of a shotgun wedding in a less than soundproof room in the middle of a busy A and E department,' she added, her shoulders slumping under the weight of yet another instance where she'd disappointed her parents. 'I can't thank you enough for getting them all to go into the interview room, but neither of my parents seemed to care enough to keep their voices down.'

'By that stage there were already enough people around to have guessed what was going on so it was probably too little, too late; the damage had already been done.' He watched her silently for a moment while she took a bite and tried to enjoy the perfect toast he'd made for her even though she knew the conversation was far from over. She could tell from the contemplative expression on his face that his formidable brain was systematically working through the situation in the same way that he analysed the far more life-threatening problems they dealt with at work.

'Well,' he began again when she was starting to wish for a way to disappear, suddenly realising that she had no right to expect anything further from him; certainly not that he would be responsible for finding a solution to the situation. As he'd reminded her parents, she was an adult, now, so what she did with her life was up to her. Not that she wouldn't welcome his input, but…

'As the saying goes, *What can't be cured must be endured*,' she commented weakly. 'The gossip will die down as soon as the grapevine latches onto something or someone else.'

'In the meantime, we're left with deciding where we go from here,' he said steadily.

'We?' she echoed, desperately trying to subdue the sudden leap that her heart gave in her chest. Was that just a slip of the tongue or did he actually envisage some sort of…what? Collaboration over the pregnancy? An ongoing relationship?

Hah! As if that was likely.

Even if she wasn't guilty of virtually propositioning him that night, he was still the man he was—Daniel Carterton, her highly successful boss and a rising star in a very

specialised field of medicine who had sex appeal to spare
and a choice of any woman he wanted. Why would he be
interested in someone that not even her parents valued
very highly when his involvement in the whole messy situation had been the result of nothing more than a one-off
emotional overload?

'Well,' he began again, his measured tone sounding as if
he was having to search for words, something that was rare
in his professional life, 'considering the fact that Colin's
involvement is at an end, and add to that your determination not to allow your parents to dictate to you...'

She groaned at the reminder. 'You do realise that my
mother hasn't given up, don't you?' she warned him. 'I
wouldn't be surprised if she employed a private detective
to hunt down a prospective groom. She'll be absolutely
mortified if she doesn't get to stage the wedding to end all
weddings for all their toffee-nosed friends, so you can bet
that she's already drawing up lists and making phone calls
to see just how quickly she can get something organised,
preferably while the pregnancy can still be disguised under
a voluminous meringue of a dress.'

'You? In a meringue dress? You'd look like the Christ-
mas fairy!' He gave a snort of laughter that would have
had her chuckling, too, if the topic hadn't been so serious.

'Don't laugh too hard,' she warned. 'You might end up
having to leave the country because both my parents have
gone away convinced that they're going to be able to get
you to tell them who the baby's father is. You mark my
words! You're going to have both of them cornering you
time and time again until you finally tell them what they
want to know.'

'You don't *honestly* think they'd do that,' he scoffed but
there was a slightly thoughtful edge to his expression.

'You'd better believe it,' she cautioned. 'Once they've

made a decision, nothing will stop them, unless you can do something to make their goal impossible.'

'You sound as if you speak from experience,' he said. 'You've come up against their determination before, I take it?'

'At school,' Jenny said, feeling slightly shamefaced when she looked back at what an idiot she'd been as a rebellious teenager. 'According to them, I had two choices of career open to me—I was either going to be a lawyer or a doctor. But preferably a doctor, to follow in the family's illustrious footsteps.'

'And?' he prompted when she paused, heartily wishing she'd never begun this topic because it certainly didn't show *her* up in a particularly good light, either.

'And the only way I could think of to make them tear up all the application forms was to deliberately fail my exams.' She shook her head. 'I'll never forget the expressions on their faces when I handed them my exam results— my utterly *appalling* exam results—and announced, "Try to force me to go to law school or medical school with *those* grades," and flounced out of the room.'

'Ah, Jenny. Talk about cutting off your nose to spite your face!' he exclaimed. 'So when *did* you get those marks I saw on your CV when you applied to work on my team?'

She blinked at the realisation that he must have read all the way through her CV to know that she must have retaken the exams at some stage.

'I approached the local comprehensive school who contacted my previous school—my very expensive all-girls boarding school—for a résumé of my marks during my last year there. Then, with my promise that I'd produce any extra course work required and would put in the necessary hours of revision, they allowed me to resit the exams with their pupils the following year, even though I wasn't attending the school.'

'What were you doing if you weren't going to school?' Trust his quick brain to pick up on that.

'I got myself a job—as a hospital cleaner—and shared the rent in a flat with three other girls. I did most of my studying at the library, where there wasn't the noise of my flatmates getting ready to go out on the town to distract me.'

'Well, knowing you managed straight As, I know it wasn't a case of not having the brains to pass the exams first time round,' he commented. 'But if it was just the fact that you didn't want to be forced into doing something you didn't want to do—'

'That is *exactly* the same situation I'll be facing again, if my parents have their way,' she interrupted, amazed to discover that the man had actually registered the grades she'd entered on her CV when she'd applied for her current post. Did he have a photographic memory that he'd retained so much?

How much more did he know about her when she knew almost nothing about him?

CHAPTER SIX

JENNY couldn't believe how lonely her little flat felt when she closed the door behind her.

Just yesterday it had felt like a sanctuary, her first home that she actually owned—well, in partnership with her bank, that was; the first place where she had complete control of what went on inside it from the simple things like choosing the colour to paint her bedroom to the more costly things like the eventual remodelling of the outdated kitchen when she could afford it.

She dropped her sadly battered handbag in her favourite armchair and walked gingerly across to the kitchen and the kettle, desperately needing a cup of tea…well, actually she'd rather have a large mug of coffee, but that was off the menu for at least the next seven or eight months, so tea it would have to be while she mulled over the changes that a single day had brought.

Just a month ago she'd been perfectly content with her life as a whole, happy with her decision to take a sideways step within the department to concentrate on mothers and their at-risk babies in the months before they were born rather than the intensive pressure of nursing those whose arrival had happened before it was safe.

It was hard to believe that everything had changed in

the space of twenty-four hours, and not just because of the results of that pregnancy test, either.

She wasn't certain, yet, whether to be grateful that Daniel's analytical mind had enabled him to put the details together to face Colin with his foul machinations. Part of her would have been perfectly happy never to have known what the man was capable of. It certainly didn't do much for her self-confidence to know that his pursuit hadn't had anything to do with love—at least, not love of *her*.

On the other hand, it had been fantastic to know what it felt like to have someone's unconditional support for the first time in her life; to have Daniel stand up for her and demand that she be accorded the right to make her own decisions. The fact that she should have done the same thing for herself...well, perhaps she could excuse herself on the grounds that she hadn't been firing on all cylinders, last night, otherwise she'd like to believe that she'd have managed to knock the idea of a rushed marriage on the head without Daniel's assistance.

Well, she hoped that was true, even though the memory of her mother's anger at her pregnancy was still enough to make her cringe like a child.

What she could be utterly certain of was that there was absolutely no way she would have ever gone through any sort of marriage with Colin, no matter how much shame and blame her parents heaped on her head. Even if she'd never found out what he'd planned to do to her, she knew she could never have married him without loving him, and she could never love him because she had already given her heart to Daniel.

'And that, in a nutshell, is why I'm standing here, in my own flat with a solitary cup of tea, talking to myself,' she said, deliberately voicing the words aloud. 'I know I could be curled up on that perfect butter-soft leather couch in

Daniel's sitting room wrapped in his dressing gown waiting for him to come back from the hospital to cook a meal
for us, but that would just be taking advantage of him.'

She allowed the words to die away because she knew
that they were less than the truth.

Yes, she *did* feel a measure of that, now that her aches
and pains were under control with the analgesics she was
taking. It *had* seemed as if she was taking advantage of
Daniel, delicious though it had felt to have him waiting on
her, hand and foot. But by far the most pressing reason for
calling a taxi to take her home was the fact that she was
afraid that she was going to be so seduced by the bone-
deep delight of knowing that he was going to be coming
back to her that she wasn't going to be able to tear herself
away from him if she stayed much longer.

So here she was, back in her own, oh, so lonely, little
domain, and already bitterly regretting her impetuous de-
parture; already kicking herself for being an idiot when
she could be enjoying Daniel's company for another night
and wondering if, when the time came to go to sleep, he
would suggest that they should share that big comfortable
bed again.

'And *that's* why you came home,' she reminded herself
with a scowl, knowing that he would have only had to look
vaguely interested in a repeat of that night a month ago
for her to eagerly agree. 'What does it say about you that
you'd be so willing to go to bed with someone who's not
in love with you?' she scolded grimly, recognising that the
fact that she was in love with him could never be enough,
not for any sort of long-term relationship and especially
not when a baby's happiness was at stake. And that was
without taking into account the fact that Daniel could have
any woman he wanted just by crooking his finger, so the
likelihood that he would want to be burdened with her

when he could have someone equally as high-flying as himself was infinitesimal.

It wasn't as if she was going to be desperate for his help in supporting the child. For all their faults, her parents would be unlikely to let the world see them abandon their only child and grandchild. Anyway, if all else failed, she could always fall back on the allowance that had been steadily mounting up, untouched, in a savings account. Pride and stubbornness had made her determined to forge her career under her own efforts, and so far she'd managed, albeit with a few spells subsisting on little more than baked beans on toast.

No, she certainly had no intention of trying to use her pregnancy to tie Daniel to her. The fact that she loved him was totally unimportant, unless he loved her, too. And as he'd obviously been keeping his distance from her ever since the night they'd spent together that clearly wasn't the case.

'So, you've got a couple more days to get your head together and then you'll be back to work and it'll be business as usual,' she lectured herself with a determined nod.

Except she had a feeling that she was only fooling herself if she thought it was ever going to be business as usual. Apart from the fact that day by day she was going to have the burgeoning reminder of her pregnancy, there was also the fact that she was never going to be able to look at Daniel without remembering the night when he'd made the rest of the world disappear.

Then, of course, she had no idea how he was going to react to her precipitate disappearance, today.

She'd written him a brief letter to thank him for his hospitality…well, her mother's years of training in the social niceties couldn't be completely ignored, especially when they were so appropriate. She really hadn't been in a fit state to look after herself last night, and it had been so nice, just for a little while, to bask in the illusion that the man she loved really cared about her, too.

The next morning, when she woke up at her usual time with the thought of two more days stretching ahead of her without seeing Daniel, suddenly her aches and pains didn't seem so bad any more.

With her decision made, she swiftly headed to the bathroom to get ready to go to work and actually arrived at the hospital nearly an hour before her shift was due to start.

'What on earth are you doing here, today?' Daniel growled under his breath when he slipped into the room and found himself next to Jenny in her usual spot during handover. 'You're supposed to be off for another two days.'

Ever since he'd arrived back at his flat to discover that his Jennywren had flown he'd been in a ghastly mood, and the sudden unexpected leap of delight that his heart had given as he'd opened the door to see her familiar face had just made his temper worse.

It was bad enough to realise that the prospect of missing seeing her for the next two days could affect him so strongly, but the significance of her leaving his flat as soon as she could had driven home the fact that she hadn't wanted to stay there nearly as much as he'd wanted her to stay; the realisation that he would have been perfectly happy if she'd *never* left.

But that was totally irrelevant to her turning up for her shift today when he knew exactly how much pain she'd been in during the night before last. He'd lain there with her in his arms and winced at every whimper as she'd moved in her sleep, guilt assailing him that she'd been the one who'd been injured instead of him. And to compound his remorse, there was the memory that he'd directed her to look after everyone else without first checking to see if *she* was injured.

It hardly mattered that the outcome for everyone in the pub had been better than anyone could have hoped with only a dislocated knee and broken wrist to add to the assorted cuts to be cleaned and sutured. That didn't excuse his negligence towards the one woman who was rapidly coming to mean the world to him.

No, much as it went against his attraction to her—and his newfound need to take care of her—it would definitely be better for Jenny if he kept his distance from her. But how could he, now that he knew about the baby she was carrying?

The baby…*his* baby… Dear God, he'd barely *begun* to take in the fact that she was pregnant, and he certainly couldn't allow himself to think about it, now, not when he was going to need every scrap of concentration to cope with a full morning's clinic, and especially if Jenny was going to be in the room with him for even part of that time.

'I remembered that it was your clinic day,' she muttered blandly, speaking softly enough not to interrupt the meeting that was just winding down around them, but his ears were so attuned to her voice that he didn't miss a word as she continued. 'I didn't want to miss out on seeing the patients I've come to know—the ones who already know me from previous visits—or seeing the new ones for the first time and finding out if there's anything you can do to help them.'

He could well understand why she would want to be there. He knew how much he looked forward to seeing how the patients were progressing, constantly delighted when progress was good and he knew he'd done his part towards bringing a healthy baby into the world. The satisfaction of such cases almost outweighed the desperate times when he was unable to work a miracle.

'You can be there *only* if you give me your word that you will tell me if you're hurting too much,' he said, torn between his concern for her and his delight that they would be working together today.

'Jenny?' Sister Rethman's voice carried easily over the buzz of conversation that followed the end of the handover. 'A word, please? Oh, and, Daniel, if you've got a minute, too?'

'I hate it when she does that,' Jenny muttered as he stepped closer to her to allow their colleagues to pass them on the way out of the door. 'It makes me feel as if I've been called to the headmistress's office to be told off for talking during assembly.'

'Did you have a lot of experience of being called to her office?' he asked, fighting to quell a grin. He could just imagine Jenny as a rebellious teenager.

'Remind me to tell you about the time I dared her to tell my parents she wanted to expel me from my mother's Alma Mater and she nearly hit me with her paperweight,' she said darkly as they approached Veronica Rethman. 'You wanted a word, Sister?' she finished brightly.

'Are you sure you should have come in today, Jenny?' her senior enquired kindly. 'By all accounts, that was a pretty nasty accident last night and you were one of the injured, to say nothing of...' She gave a meaningful glance towards Jenny's waist and once again Daniel was amazed at just how swiftly gossip could travel.

'I'm due in clinic with Dr Carterton, today,' she said, apparently calmness personified, but he could hear an edge of tension in her voice and he wondered when he'd developed the facility for reading her like that. 'It's not heavy work and I've promised to let him know if I can't cope, but I would really rather keep busy than stare at four walls for a couple of days.'

'Well, you make certain that you *do* take it easy, today,' her superior said. 'Although, heaven knows we're so short of staff at the moment and there aren't many who could step in for you. Daniel, are you sure she's really fit to do it? The hospital's insurers would have a fit if anything goes wrong.'

'I'll keep an eye on her, Ronnie,' he reassured her, crazily wishing he had the right to wrap Jenny in cotton wool to protect her. 'Was that all you wanted?'

'No. Josh asked me to pass on a message that somehow got routed through his secretary. Aliyah Farouk has asked if her husband can accompany her to her appointment later this morning, if that's all right with you? Would you like me to organise things with orthopaedics and page you when she arrives?'

'If orthopaedics are happy to let Faz off the leash, I'd be delighted for him to come with her. Has he really made *that* much progress, already?' It didn't seem so long ago that the man wasn't expected to live. Was he really ready to accompany his wife to an obstetric appointment?

'Apparently so,' she said with a quick glance at the watch pinned to her uniform pocket and a grimace. 'Anyway, I've passed on the message and I'll do the organising if you want me to. Now, the two of you had better get moving or your clinic will run later than ever.'

'Do you ever feel that you should salute and click your heels when she uses that tone?' Daniel said out of the corner of his mouth as the two of them headed towards the outpatient clinic and was delighted to hear Jenny chuckle.

'All the time,' she agreed slightly breathlessly, and he slowed his steps so that it was easier for her to keep pace with him, suddenly aware that this was the first time her surprisingly long legs hadn't been able to keep up and realising with a scowl that it must be because of the horrendous bruising she'd suffered.

'She's just one of those people who was born to organise everyone and everything,' Jenny continued with the lilt of laughter in her voice that could put sunshine into the cloudiest day. 'Some of the nurses were speculating what her house must be like. Somebody suggested that she probably lines up her herbs and spices in alphabetical order, too.'

He was grateful that the light-hearted conversation lasted all the way to the waiting area outside his room so that he couldn't be tempted to turn it to more personal topics. With the gossips already having a field day at Jenny's expense, the last thing she needed was to have someone overhear them discussing her pregnancy and the events surrounding it.

'Bring the first patient in as soon as you've checked the basic details,' he suggested before he closed the door, shutting himself into the bland office space for a few moments' privacy to review the file on the top of the teetering pile and correlate the information with the computer records. He knew that he could rely on Jenny to complete the usual checks on weight, blood pressure and so on that would be completed at any pre-natal check-up.

Sure enough, it was only a few minutes before a tap on the door heralded the first patient of the day.

'Hello, Mrs Finch. Come in and make yourself comfortable. Now, how much has your doctor told you about the reason why he's referred you to see me?' Daniel asked when the scared-looking woman had settled herself on the very edge of the seat by his desk.

'Not much,' she said nervously, looking as if she could burst into tears at any moment. 'I went for my three-month scan and they told me I was having twins but then they said they'd seen something. I don't know what they called it but it's something about transfusions and they said my babies could die.'

'Was it a shock to hear that you were having twins or are there other twins in the family?' he asked as he called up the images from that first scan and bent forward to take a closer look, using his usual ploy of sidetracking a patient's attention slightly to try to lower the tension in the room a little.

'My husband was a twin but he was the only one who survived the birth,' Amy Finch said with a glance in the petrified-looking man's direction. 'His mother said she was three days in labour and the other boy was dead by the time he was born.' She reached for her husband's hand and clutched it in a white-knuckled grip. 'That's not what's going to happen to my babies, is it?'

'We'll do our very best for your babies, I promise you,' Daniel said, aware that promising anything more than that would be cruel, especially when he didn't yet know exactly how precarious the lives of her babies were. 'And Staff Nurse Sinclair can confirm that I will always tell you the truth.'

'Even when it's something you might not want to hear,' Jenny confirmed with a wry expression. 'But at least you know that you can trust him,' she added in a totally un-expected testimonial that sent a warm wash of pleasure through him.

'In that case—' Amy Finch's husband had to swallow before he could continue '—tell us, honestly, what's wrong with our babies? Why did our doctor send Amy to you in such a hurry? What did they see on the scan?'

'Well, for a start I can tell you that your twins are iden-tical, because the problem that was spotted is something that only happens with identical twins, and even then, it's very rare. It's called Twin to Twin Transfusion Syndrome and what that means is that there are problems within the placenta—that's the plumbing that connects the babies to the wall of the uterus—problems that mean that one baby isn't getting enough blood to grow properly, while the other one is having to pump so much blood that it might damage the heart.'

'S-so they're going to d-die?' Amy hiccupped, clearly fighting tears.

'There must be *something* you can do?' her husband begged desperately. '*Something* that will keep them alive until they can be born?'

'I won't know until we've done some more tests, but it might be possible to operate—'

'You can't operate! They can't be born yet!' Amy interrupted with a wail. 'It's far too soon!'

'Of course it is,' Daniel agreed, hoping the tone of his voice would help to calm the poor woman down. Out of the corner of his eye he saw Jenny hovering, ready to comfort the distraught mother-to-be if her husband's own emotions prevented him from supplying the comfort she needed. 'If the conditions permit it, this operation would be done while the babies are still inside you, using a laser to seal off the connections in the placenta that are sending too much blood to one of the babies so that the other one can get its fair share.'

He paused just long enough to be certain that they were now following his explanation rather than panicking blindly. He still had the hard part of the task to do—covering the down side to the surgery if things didn't go according to plan.

'Of course, something like this, an intrusion into the womb at such an early stage of the pregnancy, can be very dangerous to the babies because it can trigger labour. In that case, you would almost certainly lose both babies, but because there is already a marked difference in the size of the two of them—and in their hearts—it's not an operation we can afford to put off for very long or they will die, anyway.'

'So, when will you do the operation? Can you do it today?' the young woman said, suddenly almost feverishly eager to undergo the surgery.

'Mrs Finch, we don't yet know whether an operation is possible,' Daniel warned, even as he sent up a silent prayer that it would be. 'I will need to know exactly where all the blood vessels are in the placenta and which ones are supplying which baby before I will know whether it will give one or both of them a chance of developing properly and staying alive in the womb, at least long enough to survive when they're born.'

'How soon will you know? When can I have the tests?' she demanded.

Daniel wondered if she even realised that she was stroking the swell of her belly as though to soothe the babies and reassure them. He couldn't count the number of women he'd seen doing exactly the same thing and, over the years, had idly wondered if he would ever see the mother of his own child doing the same thing, but now that he knew that Jenny was pregnant…

He was sorely tempted to glance in her direction but forced himself to concentrate.

'I can understand that you want to have the tests done as soon as possible—so do I. But even if the tests show that an operation is possible, it won't happen straight away because we're going to be doing a crucial balancing act here. If we operate too soon, before the tissues surrounding the babies are tough enough to stand being punctured and pulled around, then we'll have no chance of saving the pregnancy. On the other hand, if we wait to operate only when we're absolutely certain it's safe to do so, then both of the babies could already be too damaged and too weak to survive.'

As usual, there was a slightly stunned silence while the poor parents tried to take in the sort of detail that they'd never imagined when they first realised that their first child was on the way. He wasn't surprised to see tears trickling down Amy's cheeks as she clutched her husband's hand.

'So, we'll have all the tests and then we'll just have to wait and pray that they survive until it's safe for you to do the operation,' Simon Finch said with agony in his expression and once more Daniel had to steel himself not to be overwhelmed by the situation. This was definitely the down side of dealing with problem pregnancies, seeing the parents' desperation at first hand and wanting to do everything he could to give them what they wanted, even on the occasions when such an outcome was impossible.

'For today, we'll arrange for you to have another scan and we'll take it from there,' he said as reassuringly as he could. 'Just concentrate on taking it one day at a time and, no matter how impossible it seems, try to stay calm and think positive thoughts.'

'Stay calm!' Amy's voice rose in a wail. 'My babies could be dying and you're telling me to stay calm!'

'Mrs Finch…*Amy*, listen to me!' he called sharply, knowing it was important to attract her attention before she completely fell apart. 'I'm not being insensitive when I tell you to be calm. I'm telling you for the sake of your babies because their survival may depend on it. They are even more fragile than other babies so outside influences can have a devastating effect on them.' He gestured towards her, tense and shaking and breathing far too fast. He was glad Jenny had taken her blood pressure earlier because it was probably off the scale, now.

'Look at yourself,' he said, aiming for quiet insistence. 'Surely you must realise that the more agitated you are, the more it can affect the babies.'

'But…how?' she whimpered as she clutched the handful of tissues Jenny passed her. 'I can't just pretend that I don't know what's going on in there.'

'No one expects you to, but if your heart rate goes up, so will the babies' and that will increase the strain of coping with the effects of their faulty plumbing.'

'You could try focusing on other things,' Jenny suggested, and he was delighted that she'd jumped in at that point.

'Such as housework, or television?' Amy challenged. 'That's not likely to work.'

'Probably not, but perhaps if you were to concentrate on doing something specifically for the babies, such as reading to them or singing to them to let them become accustomed to your voice. There have been lots of studies that have shown that babies respond *after* they're born to sounds they first heard while they were in the womb.'

Both Finches seemed quite intrigued by the idea and Daniel could have hugged Jenny for making the suggestion. The last thing he wanted was to short-change the couple when they'd been bombarded with such a bombshell, and his clinics rarely ran strictly to time, no matter how hard the secretarial staff tried, but he also didn't like the idea of leaving other worried parents waiting for ever for their appointment. There were only so many times they could read the various posters on the walls, and as they'd probably been referred to him knowing there was a problem with their pregnancy, it was unlikely they would be able to concentrate long enough to read one of the magazines, no matter how up-to-date they might be.

'How are they doing?' he asked, switching his tape recorder off when Jenny came back into the room a few minutes later. At least he'd had enough time to record his notes on the problems of the Finches' pregnancy before he had time to forget anything. He was never absolutely confident that his hastily jotted notes could always be deciphered accurately should another practitioner have to see his patients at some point, so preferred to tape a spoken record that would be typed as a back-up.

'All organised,' she said with a smile. 'And tonight, they're going out for a meal to celebrate the fact that the twins are identical and to start thinking of names, both girls' and boys' because they'd rather the sex of the babies is a surprise.'

'Jenny…' His heart sank at the thought that they might be celebrating too soon. There was absolutely no guarantee that either of the babies would survive.

'And don't worry that I was giving them unrealistic expectations,' she interrupted, almost as if she'd read his mind. 'I just suggested that they should celebrate the little steps—like finding out that they were identical—so that they would be making memories they could keep, no matter how things turn out.'

He should have known from the time she'd spent dealing with the most premature of the babies on the unit that she wouldn't be one to make impossible promises. But the idea of deliberately making memories that they could cherish whether the babies lived or died could be a real comfort if worse came to worst.

'So, who's next?' he asked with a smile, musing while he waited for the next couple to enter that his high-stress job was made so much easier with someone as intelligent and compassionate as Jenny to work with.

'Sharron Pickering and her husband have been referred to us after their first visit to the pre-natal clinic. She'd been attending an IVF clinic to help her to get pregnant.'

'So, why am I seeing them?' Daniel said with a frown as he flipped the appropriate folder open on the desk. 'Surely they should be attending the assisted-reproduction unit?'

'Not any more,' Jenny said dryly. 'Sharron's pregnant, but not because she had fertilised eggs returned.'

Daniel felt his frown deepen, pleating his forehead as he deciphered her cryptic meaning, then his eyebrows nearly hit his hairline. 'Tell me she wasn't stupid enough to get pregnant when her body had been stimulated to produce eggs for harvesting! They *must* have been warned what could happen.'

She nodded dourly. 'And if what I overheard in the waiting room is true, it was done deliberately.'

'*What!*' It was a real effort not to shout. 'Why on earth would they do something so stupid? Surely they were told not to have sex because it could result in dangerous multiple pregnancies?'

'Ah, but if you're already too old to qualify for IVF in your own country and have travelled abroad for treatment, believing that this is going to be your very last possibility to ever have a child, you might be foolish enough to think that the more babies you conceive, the better your chances of ending up with at least one of them surviving,' Jenny pointed out grimly.

He closed his eyes and drew in a calming breath, reminding himself that he wasn't here to take any notice of his patients' morality or intelligence, but to focus on the health of mothers and babies.

'Well, you'd better show them in, then,' he said just as his eyes focused on one particular detail in the file.

Seven babies? The stupid woman was pregnant with *seven* babies? His anger began to soar again and it took a real effort to tamp it down as the couple came into the room with smiles on their faces.

'Mrs Pickering, take a seat, please,' he said, proud that his voice sounded relatively normal. 'I understand you've been sent to see me because there's a problem with your pregnancy.'

'Not really,' she said with a cheerful shrug. 'Apparently my blood pressure's up a bit, but that's nothing to worry about, is it?'

'Actually, it definitely *is* something to worry about,' he contradicted sharply as he took in the range of results noted in her file in less than three months. 'Your blood pressure is already astronomic and you're not halfway through this pregnancy. You're in serious danger of having a heart attack or a stroke, going into heart failure or damaging your kidneys. You could even die if something isn't done soon.'

'So, prescribe some more tablets,' she suggested airily, obviously so euphoric over the fact she was finally pregnant that she was completely unconcerned about the risks she was running. 'That's what you do for blood pressure, isn't it?'

'I would be grossly negligent if I didn't make it clear that trying to carry seven babies is not what your body is designed for,' he pointed out. 'It's a strain just for your system to keep one baby healthy because it's such a drain on your body. Seven is just…' He shook his head, searching to find words to express his thoughts without causing offence. 'To try to continue with a pregnancy of seven babies is a danger to their lives and to yours, and you should seriously think about selective reduction.'

'Selective reduction?' she echoed with a frown. 'What's that?'

'That's where we would inject into the heart of some of the babies, leaving a more reasonable number for your body to cope with.'

'You mean, you'd *kill* some of the babies? No way!' she exclaimed. 'I'm not letting you do that.'

'I know for some people there would be religious or ethical reasons why they wouldn't be happy to.'

'It's got nothing to do with religion or ethics,' she interrupted fiercely. 'They're our babies, at last, and they're all alive and I couldn't possibly do anything to any of them to...' She shook her head, unable to voice the words.

'Can't you just give her something to sort her blood pressure out?' her husband said, almost hesitantly, as if he was only now starting to realise what a dangerous situation they might be in. 'I'll make sure she takes them, and keep her off the salt.'

Daniel silently counted to ten before he turned to his computer screen and tapped in the relevant prescription, hoping that before the prescription needed renewing they might have reconsidered the situation.

'If you have any headaches or your hands and feet start to swell or—' he began, only to be interrupted.

'I promise I'll read the instructions,' Sharron said eagerly, clearly still completely oblivious to the warnings he'd tried to deliver.

'I'll come out with you to make your next appointment,' Jenny said as the two of them stood to leave and Daniel couldn't help comparing his patient's already visibly swollen body with Jenny's slender one. How long would it be before there was visible evidence of the baby growing inside her? Would she be one of those who carried the baby almost invisibly until the final trimester or would she be obviously pregnant almost from the end of the first trimester?

As crazy as it seemed when he was surrounded by pregnant women throughout his working day, somehow it felt very different knowing that it would be Jenny's body he would be watching as it grew ripe and swollen with *his* baby.

His baby! Somehow the thought still hadn't sunk in properly, but that didn't mean that he couldn't reassure Jenny that he would be there for her, would support her throughout the pregnancy and beyond; would be more than willing to be by her side for the rest of their—

'I don't think I've ever felt like smacking a patient before!' Jenny exclaimed as she re-entered the room, barely closing the door behind her before she spoke. 'I understand that the biological urge to have a baby can become an absolute obsession for some women, but she must be way beyond obsessed…crazy…mad…totally deluded if she really believes she can carry seven healthy babies to term.'

'Took a bite out of a thesaurus while you were out there making their appointment?' Daniel teased and was glad to see her smile in response. Would she still be smiling when she heard that he wanted to have a permanent part in his baby's life? And when would be the best time to broach the subject with her? Tonight, or when they'd both had a chance to come to terms with the fact of the pregnancy?

At least they had eight months to make any decisions, although as far as he was concerned, the sooner the better, especially if it meant that Jenny was going to become a permanent part of his life.

'At least we've got Aliyah coming to see us later,' her voice interrupted his thoughts, reminding him of where they should be focused. 'After Mrs Pickering, it will cheer us both up to see how well she's doing.'

'And the fact that her husband's improved enough to be able to come with her,' Daniel added. 'It looks as if they're going to have the happy ending they deserve. But in the meantime, there's this whole stack to work through, so bring in the next patient, please.'

CHAPTER SEVEN

'WOULD you rather I weren't here?' Daniel said softly as the ultrasound technician prepared to perform Jenny's first scan.

'No!' She almost grabbed for his hand, desperate not to be alone for this first glimpse of the little person who had been causing her so much grief over the past few weeks. Whoever had coined the phrase 'morning sickness' deserved to be shot, because as far as Jenny was concerned it had been 'morning, noon and night sickness'.

In fact, at one point it had been so bad that she'd actually thought of asking for something...*anything*...that would stop the constant nausea and vomiting. It had been a real problem keeping enough fluids down to prevent herself becoming dehydrated, to say nothing of trying to keep her discomfort hidden as far as Daniel and the rest of her colleagues were concerned. The last thing she needed was to lose any time off work when she was going to have a baby to support in such a short time. Anyway, she hated the thought of letting people down, be they patients or fellow members of staff.

Thank goodness, at three months almost to the day the sickness had subsided and here she was waiting to catch her first glimpse of the tiny being who had completely taken over her life, one way and another.

'I'd like you to stay, if you don't mind?' she said, belatedly realising that her wandering thoughts had gone on far too long. 'I really wasn't looking forward to being here on my own, and my parents…' She shrugged, knowing that Daniel was one of the few people who wouldn't need her to finish that thought.

'Have you got any plans for this evening?' he asked, and her crazy heart gave several extra beats at the thought that he might be going to ask her to spend some time with him, which was stupid considering she was the one who had insisted that the two of them keep a decorous distance between them. Several times he'd suggested that they should talk, but she just hadn't been ready to hear him spell out the limits he wanted to place on his involvement.

'What sort of plans?' she asked distractedly, one eye on the giant tube of conductive gel coming towards her naked belly.

'A celebratory drink—a cup of tea in your case—or a meal? It's about time we talked, don't you think?' There was something in his tone and in the intent expression in his eyes that told her that this time he wasn't going to let himself be put off any longer; that this time they would be discussing, in words of one syllable, exactly how they each saw their part in this baby's future.

Her heart gave an extra kick of apprehension, then spiked again when the chilly gel was spread over her warm skin and her squeak made him chuckle richly.

'It's funny, but until I laid down on this hard bed I hadn't really noticed that I'm already starting to get quite bulgy,' she mused, her eyes flicking from the probe stroking over the surprisingly firm little bump between her hipbones to the shadowy images appearing on the nearby screen.

'As sick as you've been, I'm surprised you aren't concave rather than *bulgy*, as you call it,' Daniel said rather pointedly, letting her know that she hadn't fooled him in the least with her attempts to pretend that all was well.

'You're reasonably certain about your dates, are you?' the technician asked, frowning at the screen. 'You did say it was just under twelve weeks, didn't you?'

Guilt brought a flush to Jenny's face as she followed the glance that the woman flicked in Daniel's direction. Much as she'd wanted him here with her—felt he had an absolute *right* to be here for that first glimpse of the child he'd fathered—she really shouldn't have agreed when Daniel said he wanted to accompany her for this appointment. He was apparently oblivious to the fact that the hospital gossips would automatically presume that his presence would signal that it was *his* baby. It would certainly make it more difficult for him to deal with the legalities of his paternity in any sort of confidential way.

'The first time you catch sight of your baby is a special occasion,' he'd insisted stubbornly, apparently oblivious to the problems he would be creating. 'Even though we're the only two who really know I have a reason for wanting to be there, I don't want you to go alone because it's something you *should* be able to share.'

'Aha!' The technician straightened up with a beaming smile. 'Well, *that's* the reason why there's already a definite bulge there,' she said, pointing at the screen. 'Can you see? There and there? That's two separate heartbeats.'

'Twins?' Jenny squeaked in shocked disbelief. 'I'm having *twins*!' She felt her eyes widen as she focused on those two bright flickering spots on the screen, evidence that there were indeed two tiny babies developing deep inside her.

Unable to help herself, she swung her gaze up to share the magical moment with Daniel, knowing that he took delight in the miracle of new life, no matter who was the

father, only there was no answering smile on Daniel's face;
no smile at all as he leaned forward to focus intently on
the shadowy images.

'Can you change the angle slightly?' he directed the
technician tersely, suddenly very much a doctor rather than
a supportive friend or a delighted father-to-be. 'I need a
better view of the placenta.'

'It looks as if there *is* only one placenta. If so, it would
definitely be identical twins rather than fraternal, with
the twinning occurring later than the first four days after
fertilisation, and the placenta *is* slightly low,' the woman
murmured as she slid the probe over Jenny's belly again,
an ominous pause sending a completely different shiver
down her spine and stopping her breath in her throat.

Almost without realising she was doing it, she found
herself reaching for Daniel's hand, desperate for the reassuring feel of his touch. For an awful fraction of a second
she was sure she felt him freeze, but before she could pull
her hand away, he immediately meshed his fingers with
hers as naturally as if it was something they did every day.

'Well, it *is* rather low, but I wouldn't have thought it
was low enough to cause placenta praevia problems,' the
technician continued and Jenny dared to breathe again.
At least it sounded as if that was one less thing to worry
about.

'Print a shot of that view and send a complete recording
of the scan to the computer in my office, please,' Daniel
directed briskly, and Jenny's heart nearly stopped. That
certainly hadn't sounded as though he wanted a copy just
as a personal memento.

'Daniel?' she croaked, hating the quiver in her voice.
It was almost impossible to speak when her mouth was as
dry as the Sahara and she was certain she was going to be

sick. She tightened her grip on his hand. 'What's wrong? What did you see?'

The technician held out a handful of tissues to wipe the gel off her belly and she was forced to relinquish her hold to accept them. On auto-pilot she wriggled her clothing into place as she slid off the couch onto legs that felt every bit as insubstantial as the blue jelly, and all the time she was waiting for him to speak...and all the time he was ominously silent.

'Thank you,' he said formally when the technician confirmed that the scan had been sent to his computer and handed him a printout, and only then did he meet Jenny's eyes. 'Let's go up to my office.'

'Daniel?' Fear had her pulse pounding loud enough for the sound to bounce off the walls. She grabbed for his elbow. 'Please. Can't you tell me what—?'

'There are other people waiting to come in for their scans, Jenny, people with full bladders,' he added with an attempt at humour that fell completely flat. The only thing it did achieve was to let her know that he wasn't going to be giving her any answers until they reached his office. But if he thought he was going to be able to put her off *then*, he had another think coming. He was going to tell her what had put that expression on his face, even if she had to lock the door and take the phone off the hook.

'Tell me,' she insisted almost before the door closed behind her, her previous desperation to find the nearest bathroom completely vanishing in the face of any threat to her baby...*babies*. 'It's something bad, isn't it? They're going to die, aren't they?' There was no point in asking the questions, really. The expression on his face as he immediately sat down behind his desk with his fingers flying over the keys to draw up the images the technician had sent was so ominous that she already knew the answer.

'Sit,' he said without taking his eyes off the screen.

'I'm not a dog!' She automatically balked at the brisk command, her response the result of far too many years of life with Douglas and Helen Sinclair as parents.

A wry twist of his mouth was probably the only apology she was going to get, especially as his focus remained on the computer.

'Sit, *please*, Jenny,' he amended distractedly, then immediately seemed to change his mind. 'Better still, come here and look at this.'

Her legs were already shaking as she made her way around the end of his desk, and when he merely leant back in his chair rather than moving away to allow her access to the screen she had to lean entirely too close to that long lean body for her senses to cope with the overload.

'Wh-what am I looking for?' she quavered, so scared that she could barely make out the flicker of the two tiny hearts that had enthralled her such a short time ago.

'The placenta,' he said shortly, pointing with one surprisingly elegant finger towards the lower edge of the image. 'As the technician pointed out, there's only one and it's attached fairly low in the uterus, but not so low that it would cause problems on its own because we both know that the uterus will stretch during the pregnancy, usually taking the placenta a safe distance away from the cervix so it won't become detached when labour starts.'

He paused the images on the screen several times to take a closer look and she'd almost reached screaming point before he began to speak again.

'It's the degree of vascularisation in the single placenta,' he murmured. 'Then there's the fact that in spite of the single placenta, the foetuses are in separate amniotic sacs and there is already a measurable difference in the size of both the sacs and of the two foetuses...' His words trailed off as he leaned closer to the screen again, his dark brows drawing together as he concentrated fiercely on detail after detail.

Jenny's sluggish brain was suddenly catapulted into frantic activity. She'd heard those exact phrases such a short time ago that it would be impossible not to recognise them or their significance.

'It's not… You *can't* be thinking it's another case of TTTS!' she exclaimed, slumping against the arm of his chair as nausea threatened and having to reach for his shoulder to brace herself against sliding ignominiously to the floor. 'It's *far* too rare to see two incidences in the same hospital within a matter of weeks of each other.' She wouldn't allow herself to think about the horrifyingly high percentage of TTTS pregnancies that ended with no live babies, or with babies so injured by their time in the womb that they could never lead a normal life.

'I couldn't be certain just from this scan,' he agreed almost absent-mindedly, his brain obviously far more concerned with picking out the first of the details that would help him to make a definitive diagnosis than choosing reassuring words to put her mind at rest, speaking to her almost as though he'd forgotten that she was the patient rather than a colleague.

'I'll need colour Doppler,' he detailed, 'to decipher exactly which way the blood is flowing in each vein and artery in the placenta to see exactly what we're dealing with…' His words tailed off momentarily then continued almost as if he was speaking to himself. 'There could be artery-to-artery, vein-to-vein *and* artery-to-vein anastomoses in there, and until we get some idea of what percentage of the blood flow is being pushed through each heart and the exact positioning of the blood vessels in the placenta, we won't know whether it will be a suitable case for surgery.'

As he'd been speaking, each detail seemed to ring a death knell for those tiny defenceless scraps. She wrapped her arms around herself, hunching forward as though curving her body around them would protect them from the disaster she could see unfolding in her mind's eye.

Her mouth was so dry that swallowing was impossible and the strange ringing sound in her ears and the difficulty she was having in focusing her eyes told her that something definitely wasn't right.

'Dan...Daniel,' she managed to stammer as a cold sweat was added to her misery, her hands trembling so much that she couldn't even raise one to touch his sleeve. 'P-please...'

'Jennywren!' she heard him exclaim as darkness overwhelmed her completely and she began to fall endlessly into space.

'Jenny?'

There was an urgent sound to the voice that was drawing her inexorably out of the darkness, and something told her that it was important not to ignore it in spite of the overwhelming feeling of dread that surrounded her.

'You're scaring me, Jenny,' said the voice that somehow didn't sound like Daniel's. 'If you don't wake up, I'm going to have to admit you to the side ward for observation and tests,' he added, then a finger that was noticeably shaking peeled back an eyelid to show her his pinched white face and reality came crashing in on her.

'Dan...Daniel?' she croaked, briefly squeezing her eyes tight shut before opening them wide to gaze up into the concern filling his expression. 'D-did I fall...hit my head?'

'Not quite,' he said gruffly, and it was only when he released his hold that she realised he'd had her hand wrapped tightly in his. 'I managed to catch you in time, before you planted your face in the floor.'

'Thank you,' she murmured and tried to use her elbows to push herself up into a sitting position only to be firmly pushed flat on the examination couch again.

'Just lie there a moment while you catch up with your-self,' he advised, hitching one hip on the edge of the couch while he watched her with eagle eyes, apparently unaware of the fact that with their thighs pressed together like that, it was the closest they'd been since *that* night.

The silence stretched uncomfortably between them, but Jenny's head was throbbing with the realisation that, no matter what turmoil they'd created in her life, she loved the two little people clinging precariously to life inside her with a fierce mother's love. The thought that either of them might not live, that they would probably only survive if she underwent a highly complex operation that even then couldn't guarantee their survival...

'I'm sorry,' Daniel said gruffly. 'That was my fault.'

His unexpected apology snapped her out of her spiral-ling thoughts.

'What was your fault?' She frowned her puzzlement.

'You passing out!' he snapped impatiently. 'I was yam-mering on about all the tests and the chances for things to go wrong and the contraindications to surgery as if you were just a member of staff rather than a patient. I should have...'

'What?' she interrupted. 'Sugar-coated the situation so I wouldn't worry?' She laughed wryly. 'Do you think, after all the details you explained about that other case of TTTS—the Finches—that I wouldn't have realised you weren't telling me everything? Do you think my memory's so bad that I could have forgotten so soon?'

'Of course not!' How had he moved so close so fast?

He'd been almost at the other end of the couch with only their thighs touching but now, there he was right beside her, reaching for her hands to take them in both of his as he leaned close enough for her to be able to draw in the delicious mixture of soap and man that was unique to Daniel Carterton. 'I know how good your memory is, Jenny, *and* the fact that once something's explained to you, you rarely forget it. But that's part of the problem.'

Those deep blue eyes seemed darker than ever when they were so close, and that reminded her all too clearly of that night when they'd been closer still. Close enough for her to have counted every sinfully long eyelash if she hadn't been far too busy exploring the rest of his delicious body to spare the time.

'Over the last few months,' he continued, apparently unaware that she was far more interested in gazing her fill than in listening to his explanation, 'I've become accustomed to talking to you…explaining things and thinking aloud as if you were another doctor. I should have remembered that too much detail wasn't appropriate this time, and put a brake on my tongue.'

'No, you shouldn't!' she objected fiercely, squeezing his hands for emphasis and loving his reassuring strength. 'I *need* to know what's going on—the good, the bad and the ugly. I know what you discovered today is about as bad as it can get, but I need to know that I can trust you to be honest with me.'

'Jenny, it might not be—'

'But most of all, Daniel,' she interrupted, 'I need you to remind me that if I hold my breath too long while I'm concentrating on what you're saying—especially when you're telling me something about me and my babies that I don't want to hear—I'm probably going to pass out.'

'You were holding your breath?' he exclaimed, clearly startled. 'What on earth for?'

'It's a habit I got into as a child.' She gave a wry smile. 'I learned that if I concentrated on holding my breath, I was less likely to argue or answer back to my parents when they were telling me off. My punishments were less, that way.'

'And you're still doing it? Deliberately?' He looked horrified.

'Of course not! I'm not stupid!' she exclaimed. 'I hadn't even realised I was holding my breath while I was looking at the scan until it was too late… I was just concentrating so hard on what you were pointing out, and what you were saying about the possibilities you could find, that—'

'Well, next time, make sure you're sitting down and concentrate a little less on the screen and a little more on breathing,' he grumbled. 'It's not good for either of us to have you passing out like that…or for the babies.'

Almost as soon as the words left his mouth, the expression on his face changed to one of dawning delight.

'It's *twins*, Jennywren!' he said softly, a wondering smile lifting the corners of his mouth and displaying the hint of dimples in both cheeks. 'We made *twins*…and identical ones, at that.'

There it was!

The sheer delight over every baby that filled this man was what had attracted her to Daniel, even more than his good looks and personality.

Just to be in the room with him at such a moment was a joy, and that was multiplied an infinite number of times now that it was her own babies—*their* babies—filling him with pleasure.

'Jenny, I think now would be a good time for the two of us to have that talk,' he said, suddenly so serious that

the first thing she thought was that he had more bad news
to tell her about her pregnancy.

'Talk?' she parroted blankly, wondering what else could
possibly be wrong.

'About the babies and the fact that I'm their father
and—'

'*No*,' she moaned, her brain and her heart already over-
loaded with the events of the last hour. '*Please*, Daniel, not
now. I can't possibly…not until we know how bad… Not
until we can be certain that they won't…'

It was obvious that he wasn't happy about the delay, but
he was a fair man and it didn't take him long to recognise
that she was in too much turmoil to make any rational
decisions.

'Okay,' he sighed heavily. 'We'll postpone that discussion till later, but it *is* going to happen, and sooner rather
than later. Now, give me a minute and I'll organise a taxi
for you,' he said, straightening up and taking several steps
away from her as though only just remembering that they
were in his office where such proximity would appear
inappropriate should anyone walk in.

'A taxi? You certainly won't,' she countered swiftly,
pushing herself up into a sitting position and swinging her
legs to hang over the side of the couch. 'There's absolutely
nothing wrong with me. *And* you've got a clinic that was
due to start seven minutes ago.'

There must have been something in her expression that
told him she wasn't going to back down, but, equally, she
could tell that, once again, he wasn't happy with her decision.

'You can stay on the strict understanding that you tell
me if you're not feeling well,' he said sternly, and she
stifled the smile that wanted to emerge at the knowledge
that he was genuinely concerned about her. The fact that

it made her feel all warm and squishy inside wasn't something she should be admitting, even to herself.

'And I'll be checking the scheduling to see how soon we can start those tests,' he added, wiping out any urge to smile in an instant. 'The quicker we know what we're dealing with…'

He didn't need to finish the thought. His consultations with Amy and Simon Finch in the intervening weeks since that first appointment were very clear in her memory. She really didn't need to have the consequences spelled out for her. The fact that her babies had so little chance of surviving was something she didn't want to think about, yet, not when she needed to concentrate on a full clinic.

Luckily, as the busy session progressed she was kept fully occupied. In a couple of cases, she had to chase up test results from the labs, in others she had to provide a consoling shoulder and box of tissues when heartbreaking news had to be broken. Best of all were the cases when she was able to join in the celebration that, against all odds, a precious baby had survived to arrive strong and healthy and a new photo could be added to the array starting to take up one wall in his office.

The session was long and tiring, especially with the recent revelations about her pregnancy preying on her mind, but she silently admitted that the need to concentrate was probably the only thing that was keeping her from going mad. If she'd been at home, waiting to find out when her own tests would be done…well, she'd probably be seven different shades of demented by now, imagining the very worst diagnosis and a dire prognosis for both of her precious babies.

She could only be overwhelmingly grateful that Daniel was turning out to be such a wonderful friend; that he was willing to stand by her. Far too many men would have disappeared into the distance when they found out about the pregnancy.

Her heart ached at the thought that he could never be more than a friend, but after today's bombshell, she couldn't be more relieved that they'd preserved a little distance between them. In a way, it would be better if he'd never known that they were his babies. He already grieved for each little life lost. How much worse was it going to be for him if he couldn't save his own children?

At least with no one other than the two of them knowing that he was the babies' father, the ethics committee wouldn't feel the need to step in to prevent him being the one to operate if it became necessary. She certainly wouldn't trust anyone else to do it.

'Earth to Jenny,' Daniel called, waving a hand in front of her face when she continued to stare into the middle distance with a worried frown drawing her eyebrows together.

He'd been growing increasingly concerned about her over the past few weeks since he'd accompanied her to that first scan, and increasingly frustrated that he couldn't do anything about his concerns.

Everything in him ached to have the right to protect her; to tell her that he loved her and hear her tell him that she loved him, too; to be there in the night to comfort her when she lay there in the darkness worrying about the precious babies they'd created.

As it was, he was trying to be grateful that she was being generous with his involvement with the daily progress of the pregnancy, beyond his clinical connection, when what he really wanted to do was sit her down and thrash out some sort of…what? A formal agreement? A legal document of some sort spelling out his rights?

No, that wasn't what he wanted. What he really wanted

was his Jennywren committed to a life together, heart and soul. Just weeks ago he couldn't wait to sit down with her and thrash everything out and he'd been frustrated when she'd wanted to hold off until her emotions were back on an even keel. Now he was glad of the delay because every day that went past, he could allow himself to believe that he would eventually get what he wanted.

Luckily, there was still time for that to happen as there wasn't any immediate urgency with the TTTS situation. Her most recent scan had confirmed that, while the smaller twin was definitely growing slower than the larger one, and the greater size of the amniotic sac was evidence of the greater volume of blood the larger twin's system was having to cope with, the situation hadn't yet reached a critical point. This was a huge relief because not only was the pregnancy not far enough along for surgery to be possible, yet, neither were the babies sufficiently developed to cope with the outside world should the operation trigger delivery.

So, given the fact that there was nothing new with her own situation...

'Sorry, I just took a call from Amy Finch,' she explained obliquely.

'She's due to come in, later this week, isn't she?' The surgery had been textbook perfect and the smaller twin had shown a remarkable gain in both size and the volume of the surrounding amniotic fluid, demonstrating that the blood volume had now increased. If they saw another few weeks of similar progress, they could be reasonably certain that both babies had a good chance of survival.

'She rang to say she'd been having contractions. I told her to come straight in,' Jenny said quietly and the reason for her pensive mood suddenly became clear.

He muttered a curse under his breath. 'Have her waters broken? Did she say?'

'They hadn't when she spoke to me, but they've got at least an hour's journey to get here, so anything could happen,' she said grimly, and with her usual smile nowhere in evidence, it was all too easy to guess where her thoughts were going and the parallels she was drawing.

His heart went out to her. As if it weren't bad enough to be carrying twins afflicted with TTTS, how much worse must it be to have another mother going through the same trauma just weeks ahead of her and for that pregnancy to look as if it had run into major problems?

'Don't borrow trouble,' he said lamely, wishing there was something, *anything*, he could do to put her mind at ease. 'You know as well as I do that every pregnancy is different, and twin pregnancies are notoriously problematic with a high rate of premature delivery.'

'Her babies aren't much over twenty-six weeks, Daniel,' she hissed heatedly, obviously aware that anyone could come upon their conversation at any time. 'That's far closer to a miscarriage than a premature delivery, and twin B has still got *so* much catching up to do.'

There was the threat of tears glittering in her eyes and he would have loved to wrap her in his arms and promise her that he would be able to keep both babies safe and well, but he couldn't do either. All he could do was take each day and each case as it came and try his hardest for every one of them.

And if she would give him the slightest sign that she wanted anything more from him than his medical expertise and a slightly distant friendship…but that obviously wasn't going to happen, now, while all her energies were focused on the babies she was carrying.

'You know we'll do everything we can to delay labour— if she really is in labour—until we can get some steroids into her to give their lungs a fighting chance, but there really isn't a magic wand I can wave to—'

'I know. I know,' she interrupted hastily, fleetingly touching her hand to his arm and sending an unexpected shower of heated sparks through his body. 'I'm sorry, Daniel, I know it's not your fault and that you want those babies to arrive healthy as much as anyone does, but... Oh! It just seems so unfair! Some women have babies as easily as shelling peas while others...'

His pager bleeped before he could comment and a quick glance at the time told him what it was about.

'That'll probably be my reminder that I should be at that wretched budget meeting,' he groaned as he reached for the phone. 'I really can't afford to miss it completely if I want to put our case for increased financing for our part of the department, but let me know as soon as the Finches arrive.'

He strode off towards yet another session that would probably degenerate into the adult version of 'you got more marbles than I did' with absolutely nothing being finalised other than the date and time of the next meeting. He knew that it was going to take all his concentration not to let his thoughts wander towards the heartbreak the Finches would suffer if they were to lose their precious babies after fighting so hard to save them.

More than that, he was so conscious of the effect the situation was having on Jenny, knowing that she probably had the same circumstances to face in the near future. It had been so obvious, when he'd taken one last quick glance over his shoulder, exactly where her thoughts were centred as she stood there with one hand protectively curved over the gentle swell of her belly, and all he'd ached to do was wrap her in his arms and make the world disappear.

* * *

It took every ounce of Jenny's skill to calm Amy Finch enough to take her blood pressure. Even then, the poor woman was sobbing broken-heartedly by the time Daniel arrived in answer to her page.

'This isn't helping, Amy!' he said sternly as he strode swiftly across to her. 'The more stressed you are, the higher your blood pressure will go and the more it will affect the babies.'

Jenny wasn't surprised that both the Finches blinked at his sharp tone, but she could understand exactly why he'd spoken that way, and the fact that they were staring at him open-mouthed and silent was testament to the effectiveness of his strategy.

'That's better!' he said in his usual calming voice. 'Now, before we start running around like chickens with their heads chopped off, let's get you on an IV and get a few results in.'

'But I'm having contractions!' Amy exclaimed. 'The babies are coming and it's far too soon and…'

'And some women have spells of contractions right through their pregnancies,' Daniel interrupted, and even though Jenny knew he was stretching a point purely to comfort the woman, she was warmed by the thought that he cared enough to try to give her some measure of reassurance. 'Give us a chance to do some tests to find out if you're one of them.'

'And in the meantime, I'll set up an IV,' Jenny said.

'Why does she need an IV?' Simon demanded. 'What are you going to be giving her?'

'Just saline, initially,' Jenny soothed. 'The last thing we need is for Amy to be dehydrated. And then, if it becomes necessary to give her any medication—if, for example, it's some sort of infection causing the problem—it will be very simple to administer immediately.' And if crossing her fingers that this would have such a simple resolution would work, she'd keep them crossed for a week, but Jenny had a nasty feeling that this was going to have a very different outcome from Aliyah Farouk's problem on the day of her husband's accident.

CHAPTER EIGHT

DANIEL had to stifle a growl of frustration when he saw how much paler Jenny's face had become over the past few days.

Knowing that she was facing such a similar situation to the Finches was obviously preying on her mind. She looked as if she hadn't slept for days—since Amy Finch was admitted, in fact—and the news this morning couldn't have been worse.

'It hasn't worked, has it?' she said sadly. 'We only managed to delay labour, not stop it…and everything seemed to be going so well after the surgery at twenty-two weeks.'

'But at least we had a chance to get some steroids into her to give the babies' lungs a better chance,' he pointed out, knowing with a heavy heart that the chances of both babies surviving such an early arrival were very slim.

Had the larger twin's system recovered sufficiently from all those weeks of overload? Had the smaller twin caught up enough to have a chance of life?

Although the parents hadn't wanted to be told the sex of their babies, he knew that the very fact that Amy Finch was carrying boys was another factor against their survival after such an early delivery.

The phone rang stridently and Jenny reached for it automatically.

'Jenny Sinclair,' she announced almost absent-mind-edly, then she straightened abruptly, almost as if she'd been stung. 'When? How far? Is everything going—?'

Daniel felt a grin lifting the corners of his mouth as he listened to her rapid-fire questions, a bubble of excite-ment giving his spirits a lift with the recognition that one of 'their' mums had obviously gone into labour. He only needed to see the smile of delight on Jenny's impish face to know that all was going well, so far.

'Who is it?' he demanded before the phone was even back in the cradle.

'Aliyah Farouk,' she said with a huge grin. 'Her labour's started early, but it's less than four weeks. Josh said to tell you that both babies have good strong heartbeats and that she's already seven centimetres dilated, and that Faz is with her in the delivery room.'

'Let me know as soon as there's any more news,' Daniel said, feeling that strange mixture of excitement and con-cern that always welled up in him with the news that one of 'his' patients was in labour. 'Heaven only knows what state I'll be in when it's my own children on the way,' he muttered under his breath as his eyes helplessly followed Jenny's progress away from him to return to Amy Finch, her still-slender hips moving in almost balletic counter-point to her shoulders as she hurried to her next task, ap-parently energised by the latest news.

She paused by the reception desk and he watched her tuck her hair behind her ear in a familiar gesture as she concentrated on the screen and desire hit him hard and fast.

It had been that way from the first time he'd met her and had only grown stronger each time he saw her smile, met her eyes, brushed oh-so-innocently against her... Dammit, everything about the woman turned him on, and the feeling was increasing exponentially as he watched her body growing ripe and round with his babies inside her. *His* babies, and they *still* hadn't had that all-important conversation, and much though he needed to have confirmation that she was going to acknowledge his rights as their father, he really couldn't justify the likelihood that such a discussion would be too stressful for Jenny while she was so worried about the babies' survival.

Something attracted her attention but when she looked over her shoulder in his direction he knew the instant when she saw him standing there—when she met his gaze—that she recognised the likely direction his thoughts had been going. The only thing he couldn't tell was what her feelings were about that direction.

'Dr Carterton?' The male voice was almost directly behind him and from the tone of it this wasn't the first time the man had spoken. It was definitely time to get his mind on the job.

'I'm sorry, Mr Finch. I really wasn't ignoring you,' he apologised and was surprised by the wry smile on the man's face.

'With pretty scenery like Jenny Sinclair around you, it's a wonder you can keep your mind on your job at all, especially when she's just such a genuinely nice person, too.' The poor man was positively grey with fatigue, every minute of the past few days showing in the discouraged slump of his shoulders. 'She's been doing her best to keep our spirits up…but Amy's convinced that both babies are going to die. Isn't there *anything* more you can do to stop her labour?'

'We've run out of options, I'm afraid,' Daniel said, gesturing towards his office as the man obviously needed to talk and the corridor was hardly the best place.

'Tell me honestly,' Simon Finch demanded almost

before Daniel could close the door to give them some privacy. 'Is there *any* chance that either of them will live?'

'Honestly? I really couldn't tell you,' Daniel said, understanding that the man didn't need or want false hope. 'For any other twins to arrive this early, I would say they had a fair to good chance, bearing in mind the improvements we've made in the care of very premature babies.'

'But *our* babies…?' he prompted. 'Is it because of the TTTS?'

'Exactly.' Daniel sighed. This was one part of his job he loathed. 'We won't know until they arrive how well they're going to cope with the outside world. Logically, the larger twin should do well, but we have no idea exactly how much damage was caused by having to cope with so much of the overall blood volume.'

'What about the smaller one…the one that was starved of blood at the beginning?'

It was hard to see his despair. It was always hard to see that emotion in a man's eyes when his dreams of a family were being snatched away from him one by one.

'Once again, we won't know until after the delivery whether—' he only just caught himself in time '—whether the baby has caught up enough to have a fighting chance.' It took some concentration to make certain he didn't let slip the fact that the babies were boys.

'I'm sorry to take up so much of your time with questions that just don't have answers,' he apologised, then caught sight of the clock on the office wall. 'Oh, my goodness! I told Amy I was going to the bathroom. She'll be wondering where I've got to, especially as she's due in theatre in a few minutes.'

'I shouldn't worry about missing anything,' Daniel teased gently. 'They won't be starting without me, so you've got time to get back to her.'

It was probably a good thing that the poor man had been absent while the epidural was being set up. Not many husbands relished the sight of needles being poked in their wife's spine, but the couple had so badly wanted Amy to be awake while the Caesarean was performed, afraid—if the worst happened—that she might miss the few moments their babies were alive if she were placed under general anaesthesia.

'You could take yourself off to get changed, ready to go into theatre,' Daniel suggested. 'That way, Amy probably won't notice how long you've been away with nothing to show for it.'

It was only when the troubled man had hurried off to follow his suggestion that Daniel allowed himself to think far enough ahead to wonder how Jenny's pregnancy would progress.

So far, although the smaller twin was gradually lagging further and further behind his brother, things had not yet reached a critical point, which was a relief because it was far too soon for either of them to survive the invasive procedure to cut the connections between their blood supplies. Any repairs this early would be like trying to suture wet tissue. Until the pregnancy went beyond the twentieth week the amniotic sac wouldn't be tough enough to survive without catastrophic leakage, and for his peace of mind he wanted it to go as far beyond as possible.

But, as ever, it would be a juggling act, balancing the safest point at which the ablative surgery could be performed against the worsening health of the babies.

His pager bleated and a quick glance told him that it would be theatre telling him everything was ready for Amy Finch's Caesarean to proceed. That meant it was time to banish all thoughts of those precious babies developing

deep inside Jenny and concentrate on the fragile beings
about to be brought into the world far sooner than was safe
for them.

'Boys!' breathed Simon Finch in a voice choked by tears
as the second baby—looking as fragile as a tiny bird—
was lifted up high enough so that they could see him
over the dark green drapes hiding the Caesarean from
their view. 'Look, Amy, love. They're boys. Two perfect
little boys.'

Daniel's heart ached for the new parents and the agony
that was to come. Their tiny sons had indeed been born
and were both alive, but for how long?

Adam, the larger twin, had been extracted first and
had initially looked healthy enough to survive. Unfortunately, the monitors revealed the struggle his organs were
making in order to overcome the damage done in those
early months.

Aidan was no better, looking so tiny and even more
fragile than his bigger brother that he seemed almost transparent and totally incapable of finding the strength to draw
enough breath to sustain life.

After the briefest of pauses for their parents to see them,
both babies were whisked off to Jenny's old domain, under
Josh Weatherby's overall supervision.

Daniel knew from what Jenny had told him about the
specialist care she'd given during her time in that department, that they would each have a nurse to monitor them
for every second of their time there, taking care of their
every need to give them the best possible chance of survival.

As for their mother, Amy's incision was swiftly closed
and, bearing in mind the fragility of the babies' condition,

it wouldn't be long before she was allowed to go to the neonatal intensive-care unit to be with them.

'What do you think of their chances?' Jenny murmured as she tried to match Daniel's long-legged stride away from theatre.

'You probably know better than I do, after your time caring for those very prem babies,' he countered. 'All I can go on is the expression on Josh's face as he was looking at them, and he didn't look hopeful.'

'They've just started off with *so* many strikes against them, haven't they?' Jenny said, trying and failing to push away the dark thought that this was the situation waiting for her in the near future.

'And you know very well that every pregnancy is completely different,' he reminded her, almost as if he had tuned in to her thoughts. 'Just because your babies have the same syndrome doesn't automatically mean that the pregnancy is going to have the same outcome.'

'It's hard not to worry when, until very recently, a diagnosis of TTTS was almost the same as a death sentence,' she said, her eyes prickling at the thought of losing the precious pair she was carrying. They might not have been planned as part of a loving, committed relationship, but that didn't mean that they weren't loved. She would do anything within her power to keep them safe. Anything.

'Has there been any news about Aliyah?' he asked and she was grateful for the complete change of topics. Her rampaging hormones made her prone to burst into tears when she saw puppies in a toilet-tissue commercial. Thinking about the dangers her babies still had to face was just too much, especially when she was on duty.

Before she could answer, his pager shrilled and he reached for the phone.

'Daniel Carterton,' he announced crisply. 'You paged me?'

'Problem?' she prompted when he put the phone back down just seconds later.

'Far from it,' he said as he set off in the direction of the delivery suites, throwing a killer grin over his shoulder that doubled her pulse rate in response. 'Aliyah's first baby has already arrived and the second one is crowning. Have you got a minute or two free? If we hurry, we could be there in time for the celebrations.'

Her break was long overdue and when she hastily reported that she was going for a coffee, she received a knowing smile and a 'Going via the delivery room?' comment followed her through the door Daniel was holding for her.

If only, she thought a few minutes later when they saw Faz Farouk carefully cradling the first of his longed-for baby boys in his arms.

It would be wonderful if she could look forward to a similar scene, with her adored husband holding for the first time the children they'd made out of their love...but it wasn't to be.

Not only was there no adoring husband, but she and Daniel hadn't even properly discussed the fact that they were *his* babies she was carrying. It was true that she was the one who'd insisted on putting off any such conversation, telling him she needed time to come to terms with the abrupt change of direction her life had taken, but he certainly didn't seem to be in any hurry to initiate it.

Was that a sign that he had no intention of having anything to do with them once they were safely born? The very thought made her heart ache, even if he did seem to be keeping a watchful eye on their development and her own health. Was there any point in hanging on any longer, hoping to see a sign that he might be interested in something more than a professional relationship with her and an arm's length one with the babies? Perhaps now was the time to sit down and talk, so that she knew his intentions and could start to plan the direction of the rest of her life.

'It wasn't so long ago that I didn't believe that this day would ever come…that I would be recovered enough to even hold them,' Faz said, speaking much more slowly than she remembered, but almost perfectly clearly.

'Well, you could hardly expect Aliyah to remain pregnant for ever,' Daniel teased.

'That's what she said.' He grinned. 'I was told I had to work hard…to be well enough to hold them before they arrived…so I could take my turns with the night feeds!'

Jenny tried to remember how many weeks it had been since that dreadful day when he'd been mown down. It was almost impossible to reconcile the broken man who had actually died several times while the surgical team had tried to put him back together with the vibrant, positive man in front of them.

Yes, he still had a long way to go, but seeing him improving so rapidly left her convinced that it was a battle he was determined to fight and win.

'Have you any idea how much longer you'll be with us?' Daniel asked. 'Will you be transferring to somewhere fairly local to continue your rehabilitation?'

'I'll be going home when Aliyah and the babies are ready to leave,' he said with a satisfied smile. 'It's one time that I'm really grateful that we're from relatively wealthy families, because our new house is almost ready…*will* be ready when we leave here.'

'Will the two of you have help with the babies?' Jenny asked, concerned for Aliyah. Caring for two newborns would be exhausting enough without also taking on the care of a man recovering from a devastating accident. 'I suppose both sets of parents will be queuing up to give cuddles.'

'They can't wait!' he agreed. 'They're also providing a live-in nanny until we get the hang of it and can cope by ourselves. And a physio to take me through my paces each day, so they installed a fully equipped gym.'

He went on to explain that the man they'd chosen would be living in, too, because he would also be assisting Faz with the everyday stuff until he was able to cope on his own.

It took nothing more than the look of determination on his face for Jenny to know that day wouldn't be long in coming. Who would have ever thought, when he was first brought into A and E more dead than alive, that just months later he should have recovered so far? Was it the fact that he'd had those precious babies on the way that had spurred his brain and body to repair so fast or was it just his single-minded perseverance, day by day and hour by hour? They would probably never know, but then, what did it matter how or why as long the outcome was good?

'Mr Farouk?' a smiling nurse called from the door of the nursery. 'Your wife has been moved to her room and said to tell you to stop being selfish with her sons. She wants to get *her* hands on them again.'

That was the ideal signal for Daniel and Jenny to take their leave, while two perfect Farouk babies were settled into a crib for the journey to their mother and Faz insisted on making the journey under his own steam.

There was just time to stick their heads round Aliyah's door to congratulate her on her beautiful babies before the little retinue arrived, and Jenny had to give herself a stern lecture all the way to the staffroom and their belated cups of tea.

There was absolutely no point in feeling jealous of the perfect little family they'd just left. The fact that Faz was still in a wheelchair was stark evidence that there were always problems in everyone's lives.

In fact, the more she thought about it, most of the problems in her own life could have been avoided if she'd just had a little more backbone.

If she was honest, she could see that she'd meekly allowed herself to be bullied for most of her life. In the case of her parents, she'd told herself that she *had* to do what they said because they had been kind enough to adopt her. Unfortunately, that meant that she had been predisposed to cave in when Colin had bullied her into going to that dinner with him. She would never know exactly what he'd been planning, thank goodness, because Daniel had appeared from nowhere, like her own personal knight in shining armour, and made certain she was safe.

She smiled up at Daniel to thank him for the mug of tea he offered as a revelation suddenly burst inside her.

Daniel was the only person who had never tried to bully her.

In fact, having him at her side during that awful confrontation the night of her accident was the first time she'd openly defied either of her parents. Throughout her childhood and almost to the present day, whenever her wishes had gone contrary to theirs, she'd tried to find some way of achieving what she'd wanted by sleight of hand rather than arguing with them, even though she knew that she would once again be disappointing them.

It was all too obvious that her mother had been angry that their daughter wasn't willing to do whatever was necessary so that the family name remained unsullied, and Jenny was ashamed to admit that she'd only summoned up the courage to refuse to submit to her parents' dictates because she'd been able to feel Daniel's silent support.

It had been an absolute revelation to actually have someone angry on her behalf rather than angry with her, but she had yet to use the new confidence it had given her to tell Daniel that she was ready to sit down with him and really talk about their situation and what would happen after the babies were born.

'I've been thinking…' Daniel said a little more than a week later.

The department was only just settling down after a visit from Aliyah and Faz to show off their perfect babies before they left for their new home, and Jenny would have been lying if she said her heart hadn't ached at the perfect picture they'd made.

As per hospital regulations, each of them had been sitting in a wheelchair, but with each parent cradling a bundle swaddled in a pristine white shawl that contrasted beautifully with a thick cap of dark hair—already showing a tendency to curl—there wasn't a member of staff who hadn't stopped to coo and offer misty-eyed congratulations.

Faz's parting shot before they'd been driven away had been to joke about the hospital's infamous parking.

'In a way, it was a good job we'd caught a cab to the hospital that day,' he said with that slightly lopsided grin. 'If I'd driven here and parked in the car park, the parking charges would have bankrupted me by now.'

Jenny smiled at the memory of the burst of laughter that had followed their vehicle and the resulting lift in her spirits prompted her to tease Daniel into displaying those sexy dimples again.

'Is this a new thing?' Jenny asked, cheekily, as she

kicked her shoes off and turned in her seat to settle her feet
onto the chair opposite. At his quizzical look she elabo-
rated. 'You said that you've taken up thinking. Is that a
new thing?'

'Ha!' He threw a crisp at her which she caught in midair
and promptly popped into her mouth to crunch with noisy
relish. 'I was actually trying to initiate a serious conversation,' he complained as he lifted her feet out of the chair so
that he could sit in it then startled her by depositing both
of her feet in his lap where he proceeded to press both
thumbs firmly into the aching muscles and ligaments in
the arch of one foot.

'Oh, yes!' she groaned with a mixture of agony and
bliss. 'Forget about talking. Just keep doing that to my feet.
They're starting to complain loudly about all this weight
I'm putting on.'

He continued in silence for several minutes, alternating his ministrations from one foot to the other until she'd
almost melted in a puddle, amazed that she'd never realised
before that the soles of her feet could be an erogenous
zone...in the hands of the right man.

Unfortunately, she and her hormonally overactive erogenous zones might see him as the right man, but cold hard
logic told a different story.

In fact, the longer the pregnancy went on, the guiltier
she felt about the situation she'd created that never-to-be-
forgotten night. If she hadn't fallen apart on him, then
offered herself on a plate, making it virtually impossible
for a red-blooded man like Daniel to turn her down...

The fact that he'd kept a very proper professional distance between them ever since was proof enough that
he had no interest in pursuing any sort of ongoing relationship with her. Well, why would he when he could
have any woman he wanted, and there were plenty of

high-fliers—doctors and consultants in this hospital, alone—who would have taken him up on an invitation in a flash.

As it was, if it weren't for the fact that she was pregnant, she could probably have put the events of that night to the back of her head, too. At least, one day she might, when she didn't relive them in heart-thumping detail night after night. The fact that she sometimes fooled herself into thinking that she saw desire in his eyes when she caught his gaze was nothing more than wishful thinking.

'As I said, Jenny,' Daniel began again, squeezing one foot in each hand to get her attention and dragging her thoughts out of their interminable circles, 'I've been thinking, and it seems to me that the most logical thing would be for the two of us to get married.'

Jenny stared at him in disbelief, certain she must have misheard him, or that he'd found a novel way to tease her.

Totally unable to find a single word to say, she just gazed at him. Numbly wondering if her mouth was hanging open she fought to take a breath, her heart hammering insanely as she registered the strange watchful seriousness of his gaze.

'Well?' he prompted, and if she hadn't felt the tension in the hands still gripping her feet, she might have believed that he was as relaxed and laid-back as ever.

'Well, what?' she managed, her voice sounding strangely strangled as an enormous bubble of hope started to inflate inside her chest. If the man who'd stolen her heart the first time she'd caught sight of him all those months ago was about to tell her he was in love with her, she'd leap into his arms so fast it would make both their heads swim. And the fact that her pregnancy was already making getting out of chairs cumbersome and ungainly wouldn't stop her, either.

'Don't you think it's the most logical step?' he asked, sounding so horribly matter-of-fact that deflation was almost instant.

'Why is it logical?' she managed, even as a leaden ache took the place of that short-lived bubble of ecstasy. There was nothing like being brought to earth with a bump to burst flimsy bubbles.

'Well, you know as well as I do that things can go wrong with "problem" pregnancies, and they don't come much more high-risk than TTTS.'

'And?' Her stupid heart couldn't give up if there was the slightest possibility that he might tell her that he wanted to be there for her…not just because of the pregnancy but for ever, because he lov—

'Because I want to be there for you,' he said, almost as if he'd heard an echo of the words inside her head. 'Every pregnant woman should have a partner—*someone*—at her side for support, for encouragement.'

Her spirits plunged again then dropped deeper still when he continued in a more serious tone. 'Then there's the possibility—rare though it is these days—that something might happen to you.' He hesitated a beat, as though weighing up the advisability of his next words. 'You haven't said much about your own childhood, but from what you *have* said, well, I don't think you'd really want to take a chance that your parents might end up taking responsibility for—'

'No!' she exclaimed far too loudly, trying to silence the cacophony in her head. She certainly *didn't* want her parents to take charge of her babies. If she wasn't around to show them all the love they deserved, herself, the *last* thing she wanted was for them to be brought up in the same atmosphere that she'd had to endure, always trying so hard to gain the approval that never came. It had taken far too many unhappy years before she'd finally admitted that she was never going to be the perfect child they'd wanted; the child they'd thought they were getting when they'd adopted her.

'I'll write a will,' she said into the startled silence, unable to believe her eyes when she thought she caught a glimpse of pain in his eyes. 'I'll make certain that, if anything happens to me, they'll go to a good home where they'll be wanted and loved, not just tolerated for the sake of appearances or because they're the means of perpetuating the family name for another generation.'

'And what about me?' he asked quietly, his face so expressionless that she had absolutely no idea what he wanted her to say.

'Well, obviously, the last thing I want is for you to have to take the children on. They'd be a constant reminder of… of…' She could feel the heat building in her cheeks as she tried to find an acceptable way of bringing up the fact that she'd taken advantage of his caring nature that night, falling apart on him and then seducing him. It would add insult to injury if he ended up with the burden of raising the children that were the result of her actions.

'Well,' he said quietly, his expression totally blank, 'I made the offer and I meant it. If you should change your mind…'

Jenny knew exactly why she felt so much like crying. The man she loved was offering her everything she'd dreamed of. Everything except the most important part— his love. Without that, marriage would be meaningless.

And if she felt herself weakening—felt tempted to marry him in the hope that she had enough love for both of them—all she had to do was remind herself of the most important reason why she couldn't take him up on his offer, that if he married her before the babies arrived, he wouldn't be allowed to operate, and she didn't trust anyone else to save her precious babies.

Daniel felt as if he'd been gutted like a fish, left with a huge aching hole where his heart should be.

He knew he hadn't made a very good job of suggesting that they could get married, but it was something he'd never done before. He hadn't even remembered to tell her that he was in love with her, for heaven's sake, although that might have been a bit of a stroke of luck, as it turned out. Having his marriage proposal turned down in such a way certainly hadn't been pleasant—dammit, it had hurt as badly as a knife between the ribs—but at least he hadn't had his love thrown back in his face at the same time. That would probably have been the final straw for his ego.

He'd honestly believed that the two of them had a friendly enough rapport that she would have been willing to discuss the possibility of marriage. He'd have to be blind not to recognise the electricity that sparked between them as strongly as ever, even though he was well aware that she wasn't in love with him.

He'd even been grimly prepared for the possibility that she might accept for the sake of the babies with the proviso that it would be a platonic relationship, although with his X-rated dreams that would probably have killed him. The last thing he'd been prepared for was a flat *no*, even when he'd brought up the possibility that the babies might end up with her parents. And her suggestion that the babies—*his* babies—would be better off with another couple...

'What a mess!' he groaned, raking his fingers through his hair then clenching them tight so that the sharp tug on the roots gave him something else to focus on apart from his own stupidity.

As if he didn't already feel guilty enough for taking

advantage of Jenny when she'd been in such an emotional state, but he'd been so attracted to her, right from the first moment he'd seen her walk into the department. If he was honest, he had wanted her so much that it was impossible to regret that one perfect night, in spite of the fact that it had resulted in such a high-risk pregnancy and probably derailed her career.

For weeks, now, he'd been all too aware that she'd been doing her best to keep a certain distance between them, but that hadn't stopped the sharp awareness building between them so that sometimes it felt as if there should be an audible crackle in the air.

Added to that was the fact that his concentration was deteriorating badly. It was fine when he was with a patient because his professionalism kicked in, but the rest of the time it was becoming increasingly difficult for him to think about anything other than Jenny and the precious babies she was carrying, especially as she was so obviously worrying, too.

Nothing had given him peace of mind until he'd convinced himself that she would welcome a proposal of marriage as a way of guaranteeing that there was no question about the babies' security should anything ever happen to her. The fact that by giving her that protection he would be marrying the woman he loved and desired above all others…

'So, what are you going to do about it, man?' he growled, then blinked as his words came back at him in the confines of his office, only then realising that he'd spoken aloud. At least he hadn't left the door open where anyone could have heard him as they'd passed by. *That* wouldn't have done his reputation much good.

As if he cared about his reputation when all he could think about was finding some way of persuading Jenny to change her mind. He couldn't do anything to change where he'd come from, but perhaps if he could engineer some off-duty time together, he could show her that he was something more than the boy from the wrong side of the tracks, now; that he was a man she could trust to take care of her and her babies simply because he loved them, whether she ever returned that love or not.

He certainly wasn't going to meekly accept her refusal at face value, not until he'd done everything he could to find out if there was any way he could persuade her to change her mind. He was so busy contemplating ways of bringing that about that he almost didn't hear the hesitant knock at his door.

CHAPTER NINE

'I'M SO sorry to disturb you,' Amy Finch apologised from the doorway, apparently unwilling to come right into his room even with an invitation. 'I know how busy you are and I really don't want to waste any of your time, but...'

'You're very welcome,' he said with a smile even as he catalogued her darkly shadowed eyes and her unhappy expression.

He knew her babies were still clinging precariously to life in SCBU but it was obvious that she had something on her mind.

'You're rescuing me from having to plough my way through a Mount Everest of paperwork. Would you like a cup of tea or coffee?' he offered, wondering how on earth he was going to get the poor woman to relax enough to talk.

'Oh, no!' she exclaimed hastily. 'I wouldn't want to put anyone to any trouble.'

'*Please* say you want one,' he whispered mock-confidentially. 'Then that means I can have someone bring one for me, too.'

At least that teased a half-smile out of her and she nodded and said, 'Tea, then, please,' as she perched on the very edge of the seat he'd gestured towards as he picked up the phone.

By sheer coincidence it was the very person who'd been occupying so much of his thoughts of late who answered, with a cheerful, 'Hello, this is Jenny. Can I help you?'

'I hope so,' he said, then paused to clear his throat when he heard how husky he sounded before continuing. 'Could you bring three teas, Jenny, if you've got a minute?'

'Of course I have,' she said and he wondered if it was just wishful thinking that made him hear a different note in her voice now that she knew who she was speaking to. 'I'll be there in a jiffy.'

Knowing they were going to be interrupted shortly, he kept the conversation to the mundane topics of the weather and the traffic chaos being caused by the contractors building a new block of 'high-quality apartments' not far from the hospital entrance.

Amy tried to respond but she looked fragile enough to shatter at the slightest thing and jumped visibly when Jenny's head poked around the door.

'Three teas, as requested,' she announced cheerfully, balancing the tray on the corner of his desk to deliver his cup before turning to Amy. 'Shall I give Simon a call to tell him to get it while it's hot?'

'Simon's not here at the moment…he's had to go back to work. He said he's afraid he'll lose his job if he has any more time off. He's trying to save some days for when… in case…' With a wail she dissolved into a flood of tears.

Daniel hadn't realised that the poor woman was quite so close to collapse and sent up a silent word of thanks that Jenny was here, especially when she immediately knelt beside Amy and wrapped comforting arms around her, rocking her gently while she sobbed on Jenny's slender shoulder.

'I've been visiting them every day, doing what I can for

them, or just talking to them. But all I can think of is how small they are and how sick and…and…'

Daniel expected Jenny to murmur comforting words to help the poor woman to calm down, but when she stayed silent, allowing all the agony and misery to pour out, he realised that her instincts were better. Amy needed to vent it all out of her system, rather like lancing a boil to release the trapped poison.

'And Simon…' Amy wailed afresh. 'Poor Simon…'

The man had been so excited when he'd been told they were expecting twins. Daniel could imagine only too clearly how he must be feeling knowing that he could lose one or both of them at any moment.

'You need to be strong for each other,' he heard Jenny murmur and his heart ached that she wouldn't let him be there for her while she waited and worried about the two boys going through exactly the same life-threatening circumstances inside her. 'He didn't carry the babies, but they are his babies as much as they're yours so he's just as worried as you are.'

'But that's just it!' Amy sobbed. 'I feel so guilty that I failed him—that I wasn't able to give him the strong, healthy family we wanted. And I know that if Adam and Aidan don't live, I'll never be able to bear to have him near me, to touch me. I love him desperately, but I couldn't bear it if this happened all over again.'

'Amy, that's one thing you *don't* have to worry about,' Daniel interrupted for the first time. 'We've explained to you—several times, both during your pregnancy and since—that the chances of another TTTS pregnancy are astronomically small. At the time you were probably far too overwhelmed by everything to listen and take it in, but it's time to try again, to tell you that any future pregnancies will probably be quite boringly normal, as far as pregnancy can ever be boring.'

'But…'

'I know this is hardly the moment to be talking to you about future pregnancies—when your body hasn't recovered from this one and your two little boys are still fighting to grow big enough and strong enough for you to take them home…'

'But it doesn't seem as if that's *ever* going to happen,' Amy wailed, 'and they just look so *lonely* in their separate incubators. It seems as if Adam and Aaron should be there together, the two of them together in the cot, the way they were inside me…'

'Have you suggested it to the staff in the unit?' Daniel asked.

'I didn't like to. I don't know them as well as I know the two of you, and I wouldn't want them to think that I was criticising them, or anything.'

'That *won't* be a problem,' Jenny said firmly. 'I used to work in that unit, and if a parent had a workable suggestion, Josh Weatherby and his staff are always open to new ideas. Of course, if there's a medical reason why the two of them *can't* be together, you can be certain they'll explain it to you.'

Amy's face was a mixture of sorrow and dawning hope, and Daniel almost swore aloud at the interruption when the telephone rang, until he heard the message being delivered.

'Amy, Simon's looking for you down in NICU,' he reported with a smile after a slightly cryptic conversation. 'He needs you there to celebrate.'

'Simon? In NICU? To celebrate?' Daniel completely understood the way she was having trouble stringing two thoughts together. He'd seen it happen too many times for it to surprise him any more.

'Apparently, he arrived just after you left. He came back because he'd just had an idea—he wanted to suggest that the boys should be put into the same incubator.'

'And?' Jenny prompted, knowing from Daniel's expression and the glint in those beautiful sapphire eyes that there was more.

'And, almost immediately they were settled in side by side, they reached out for each other.'

'And?' This time it was Amy asking.

'And the monitor readings are already looking better... stronger,' Daniel told her, delighted to see the dawning look of hope that spread over her tear-ravaged face.

'I must go to them,' Amy said breathlessly, then paused. 'Oh, I must look a sight!'

'Take a quick detour through the nearest washroom and splash some cold water over your face,' Jenny suggested with a smile. 'And as soon as you see Simon give him a hug—he'll probably be too busy hugging you back to notice if your nose is a bit pink, and by then you'll probably both be crying.'

'I'm so sorry for taking up so much of your time... both of you,' Amy said as she scrambled to gather up the crumpled tissues. 'I can't thank you enough for listening and for not sending me on my way with a flea in my ear—'

'We'd *never* do that!' Jenny exclaimed, clearly horrified at the idea, only just beating him to the punch.

'Any time you feel you need to have a word—either because you've got problems or because you've got good news to tell us—feel free to come over,' Daniel said and smiled as his last words followed the rapidly disappearing body hurrying towards NICU.

'You were so good with her—'

'How did you know what to say to her?' Daniel's question clashed with Jenny's compliment, and while her praise wrapped warm fingers around his heart, he didn't really feel he'd done anything special. 'How did you know that she needed to let it all out; that you should just hold her and wait?'

She was silent for a moment, her head tilted slightly while she thought. 'Sometimes it's just a case of asking myself what I would like someone to do for me in a particular situation.' She frowned briefly then grinned at him. 'Perhaps it's that infamous feminine intuition that tells me when a hug will do and when someone needs words of consolation or words of wisdom.'

'And that's what you would have wanted in the same sort of situation?' He suddenly realised that he was learning more about this complex, fascinating woman all the time.

'It's a scary thought that I might be in exactly the same situation in a few weeks,' she said, all signs of that cheeky grin vanishing as if it had never been. Now there were shadows in her eyes; shadows that he would love to be able to banish, but even if he could think of a way, Jenny probably wouldn't let him close enough to try.

Daniel remained sitting at his desk after she'd hurried off on some unnamed task, marvelling that she was every bit as energetic as ever, in spite of the fact that she was already carrying extra weight and her centre of gravity had dropped with her expanding waistline.

He marvelled that she was still just as slender from the back as ever; as lean and elegant as a ballerina. It was only when she turned that you could see the bump swelling out the front of her uniform, as often as not with her hand resting on it or stroking gently over it.

With a series of clicks he was able to access Jenny's file and bring up the images of the latest scans that showed all too clearly the worrying disparity in the sizes of the babies, worrying and increasing with each new scan, telling him that the point of no return was approaching fast.

He'd hoped that, as sometimes happened, the smaller twin would manage to develop enough—albeit at a slower rate than his bigger brother—so that they could avoid the dangers of surgery. This obviously wasn't going to be one of those times.

'So tiny,' he groaned and stared down at his clenched fists on the blotter wishing there was something he could do...*anything*...to hasten the day when it would be safe to operate. He turned his hands over and stretched them out flat, mentally comparing the length of each tiny body with the distance from fingertip to wrist. 'I could hold one of them in each hand, and the two of them together would hardly weigh the same as a bag of sugar.'

Tears burned the back of his eyes at the thought that he might never have the chance to hold them if they didn't live. They were already little people to him, from the very first second he'd caught sight of them on the ultrasound screen, and the hold their tiny starfish hands had on his heart would never go, no matter what. If anything happened to them, it wouldn't only be Jenny's heart that was broken.

Then an alternative scenario flashed into his head—the one that almost stopped his heart completely every time it tried to surface—and he knew that pushing it to the back of his mind just wasn't going to work any more. It was something that he had to confront on a regular basis, working in his specialty, even though it didn't happen very often, but because the babies she was carrying were his babies, too, he was going to have to bring it up again... What would he do if something should happen to Jenny? What would happen to those precious babies if they survived and their mother didn't?

'I *can't* leave it much longer,' he declared aloud and just hearing the words made the decision firmer. The latest scans still showed that it was going to be necessary to perform the ablative surgery, but before that happened, he was going to have to sit Jenny down and insist that they discussed their options.

Discussed their options?

'Hah!' He certainly wasn't laughing because he could just imagine how that 'discussion' would go. Jenny had far too many years of fighting her corner against domineering parents to ever meekly submit to anyone else trying to dictate what she should do with her life. He was going to have to tread very carefully along the line that separated telling her that he was in love with her and wanted to marry her with or without the babies, and pointing out that she needed to have someone with the legal right to take over the care of those babies in the event that she was unable to.

And he was a crazy fool that the mere thought that their discussion might end up with her falling into his arms and declaring she loved him too was enough to send his pulse galloping.

Jenny glanced at her watch then at the large clock on the wall, marvelling at the fact that the hands were moving so slowly when she was so jittery with nerves that it felt as if she could run a marathon at the speed of light.

He only offered to give you a lift home because it's raining, she reminded herself, cross that she'd actually tried to read anything more into the suggestion. A highly qualified consultant like Daniel Carterton certainly wouldn't be as uncertain or nervous as a teenager about offering a lowly member of staff a lift in his car when they were going to be travelling in the same direction. And the fact that he'd seemed to be watching her surreptitiously was probably nothing more than her imagination.

She certainly didn't have any reason to build his offer up into anything special; after all, despite that one unforgettable night and the fact that he was her babies' father, the two of them were nothing more than friends, now. The fact that her skin tingled and her heart took off at a gallop whenever he was near, and that she was tempted to grab hold of Daniel and hold on for all she was worth, made her feel dreadfully guilty because he deserved to fall in love with the woman he wanted to marry, not just to marry because it was 'the right thing' in such a situation.

'I couldn't do that to him,' she murmured fiercely, even though she would love to have Daniel as a permanent part of their lives. And if he should meet someone else and want a divorce...how much greater would her heartache be then?

Afraid that her tongue might give voice to the argument going on in her head—the course that she knew was right versus the one she wanted to take—she didn't dare sit in silence during the ride.

She didn't want to bring up something as depressing as the news that had been relayed to them that Sharron Pickering's gamble hadn't paid off—that she'd lost all seven of the babies she'd been carrying. Sadly, complications meant it had also been necessary for her to have a hysterectomy to save her own life, so there would be no further chance for her to have the baby for which she'd been willing to risk everything.

In a quiet corner of the staffroom a little while later, she'd come across Daniel hunched forward in one of the less comfortable chairs with a cup of cold coffee suspended between his knees, the knuckles of both hands bone-white as they clenched around the sturdy pottery.

Immediately, she'd been certain she knew what was on his mind and had paused beside him with her back to the room to minimise the chance of their conversation being overheard.

'You can't afford to let it get to you,' she'd murmured quietly. 'The Sharron Pickerings of the world just aren't worth getting upset over when there are so many other women who need and want your help enough to respect your advice and follow it.'

'That doesn't stop me from...from *grieving* for those seven babies. None of them ever had a chance to be born and draw their first breath,' he'd growled. 'Of course it's sad that a woman's obsession to have a baby nearly destroyed her own life. I'm finding it difficult to be sympathetic when it was entirely her own fault, but those babies...' He'd shaken his head and in spite of the poor light in this corner of the room, Jenny had been certain she'd seen the glitter of the threat of tears in those dark sapphire eyes before he'd looked back down into the unappetising liquid in the mug he was holding.

No, that really wasn't a topic she wanted to resurrect in the close confines of his car. There must be something else she could bring up that would break the strangely tense silence that stretched between them.

'Your patience with that last patient in the clinic certainly paid off in the end,' she said, finding a topic that would keep her out of mischief without depressing them both in the process. According to her notes, Susan Feldman had been very overweight at the time of her first appointment at the hospital, and had been very resistant to the idea that losing weight would make any difference to her chances of achieving the pregnancy she longed for. 'She was absolutely over the moon...both with her weight loss and with the fact that she'll shortly be putting some of it on again, now that she's pregnant.'

'She deserves all the credit for sticking to her diet,' he said. 'I didn't do it for her.'

'But, according to her, you were the first one to sit down and take the time to point out the probable connection between her weight and her inability to conceive, and to encourage her to do something about it without preaching and wagging your finger.'

'Sometimes I even surprise myself,' he said dryly, and the wry grin that tilted his mouth drew her gaze in the half-light and made her wish she could see it more clearly. Better still, she wished she could taste it again. One night really hadn't been enough to do more than whet her appetite for more of the same.

'I think one of the things that stuck with her was the fact I told her that very skinny woman can have similar problems, including early onset menopause.'

'Do you think it's a form of self-preservation that a significant number of women who are considerably over-weight or underweight can't get pregnant...or can't carry a baby successfully if they *do* manage to get pregnant?' Jenny asked, always eager to learn. 'Do you think that their bodies are already having a struggle to cope with day-to-day living, so they're unable to carry a baby to term?'

'There are just so many potentially awful consequences for pregnant women who aren't otherwise taking proper care of themselves. You mentioned the potential for early onset menopause for underweight women, preventing them from ever conceiving a child, but at the other end of the range there's a whole raft of other dangers...gestational diabetes, eclampsia—'

'You hardly need to list them for me,' she pointed out with a chuckle. 'When I was working in SCBU, I regularly saw babies born far too soon because their mothers weren't able to carry them any longer. And a rising number of those mums were women who were either stick thin or were already grossly overweight *before* they got pregnant.'

He sighed heavily. 'I just hate seeing innocent babies die when it's so unnecessary and so preventable. All the women have to do to prove how determined they are to have a baby is to get themselves healthy by changing their diet and taking a sensible amount of exercise. It's not rocket science, just sensible calorie counting and no cheating. And when they finally hold that baby, they'll *know* it was all worthwhile.'

'There speaks someone who's obviously never had a problem with his weight,' she teased, glad he had no idea just how often she daydreamed about the gorgeous naked body she'd explored that night; a body that was all long, lean, power-packed muscles without a trace of flab in sight anywhere. 'I can personally vouch for the fact that an un-happy, lardy, ungainly teenager with an unhealthy taste for junk food can grow up into a pretty hefty adult. It took me nearly two years to finally sort myself out, probably because I started off with a severe lack of will power and an absolute craving for anything containing monosodium glutamate.'

'Well, you certainly don't look as if you've ever had a problem,' he countered gratifyingly swiftly. 'You're slim, but without being so skinny that you look as if you could snap like a twig. Even now, at six months pregnant, you're not carrying any surplus weight. In fact, you look as slen-der as ever from the back.'

And he'd been looking? Just the thought of it had a blush heating her face at the same time as a warm glow curled around her heart. He'd noticed her body and had been admiring it in spite of the fact that she was about to start the third trimester of a twin pregnancy?

'Thank you for the compliment,' she managed, huskily. She was relieved to note that they'd reached the front of the house she currently called home and wondered how the innocuous conversation she'd started to fill the journey had ended up turning so personal. Still, they were here now and soon she'd be able to hide the volatile mixture of pleasure and embarrassment behind her front door.

So, why did she hear herself offering to make him a coffee when she should just have thanked him for the lift and hurried in out of the rain?

'You've probably had more coffee than is good for you already today,' she hastily backpedalled, but it was too late. He'd already switched the engine off and was climbing out of the car.

'Hang on. Plan B,' he said over the sound of the rain hitting the car roof as she scampered up the short path through the puddles. 'Shall I whip up to the shop at the end of the road and pick up some fish and chips? Or would you prefer Chinese, or Indian?'

'Not Indian,' she said with a shudder from the dubious shelter of the inadequate porch. 'Ordinarily, I love it, but at the moment it gives me wicked heartburn.'

'And I'm always starving an hour after I've eaten Chinese, even if I've been a glutton, so that makes it fish and chips, then,' he said with a grin. 'I'll be back in five minutes, just enough time for you to make the tea.'

Jenny wasn't quite sure how he'd demolished any trace of her determination to keep her distance from him. Probably it was the fault of that grin and the way her imagination was trying work out how much damage it would do to her heart if she had three identical grins to contend with on a daily basis.

'Oh, but I would love it if they *did* have his grin,' she whispered with a catch in her throat as she grabbed cutlery from the drawer and sandwiched a sheet of wet kitchen towel between two plates and set the microwave ready to switch on when Daniel returned so they wouldn't have to put their food on cold plates.

'And if I could be setting the table like this on a daily basis, ready for when he comes home at the end of his shift… Whoa! What am I *saying*!' she exclaimed when she realised she'd sounded as if she was ready to throw away all her hard work in building her career to stay home and play happy families. She'd had to study far too hard and had to battle against the wishes of her parents for too many years to give up her dream so easily.

'And anyway, there's no guarantee that either of the babies will survive,' she reminded herself in a tight whisper, 'and there's certainly no guarantee that Daniel would still be interested in me *without* them.'

After her stern reminders to herself, their meal was unexpectedly relaxed, their conversation ranging far and wide the way it always had in the days before *that night*.

It was only as Daniel was rinsing the plates off at the sink, having insisted that she put her feet up while she got the chance, that it became more personal again.

'How have you been feeling?' he asked casually…as if there could ever be a casual question about the babies that he'd fathered that unforgettable night. 'Are the two of them starting to kick you black and blue?'

'At least one of them is going to be a footballer, or a flamenco dancer,' she joked and rested her hand on top of what was already a pronounced bulge. 'Of course, the activity is always worse when I'm lying in bed, and any time I sit down for more than two minutes.' She paused, waiting for the next sign of activity and wondering whether it would be an elbow or a knee this time, and whether it would be right up under her ribs or on her poor battered bladder...except the activity didn't come.

'That's odd,' she said as she smoothed both palms over the tight hard curve, exploring and tracing outlines to see if the babies had managed to settle themselves in a position that would mute their activity. 'They're not usually so quiet at this time of night. They're real night owls...'

She started to feel queasy, worry making her supper feel like lead in her stomach as she tried to remember exactly when she'd last felt any movement.

'Daniel?' Something in the tone of her voice must have alerted him because he immediately whirled to face her.

'What is it, Jenny?' he demanded, dropping to his knees in front of her, his deep blue eyes darkening still further as he slid both hands between hers, his long fingers almost completely spanning the bulge of her pregnancy as he spread them wide. 'Are you in pain? You're not having contractions, are you?'

'No. Daniel, they're not moving!' She placed her hands over his and pressed them tightly against her belly. 'The babies aren't moving and I can't remember when they last kicked me. I don't know how long ago...' Panic robbed her of further words and she could hardly see the horrified expression on his face for the tears flooding her eyes.

The next hour passed in a blur.

She couldn't remember travelling to the hospital at all, and even though she tried her hardest to take note of everything going on around her—knowing how crucial a single finding could be—it was almost as if she had been isolated in a bubble with her terror so that nothing else could get through to her.

Nothing but Daniel.

All he had to do was touch her and she felt connected again, grounded and somehow protected at the same time.

She knew that it was stupid, but she'd somehow managed to convince herself that as long as Daniel was there with her, nothing bad could happen to her precious babies.

Then he crouched down in front of her and took both her hands in his, and just the seriousness of the expression on his face was enough to tell her that he was there to give her bad news.

For a crazy moment she wanted to pull her hands away and put them over her ears so he couldn't say the words that would break her heart, but she'd never been a coward. Anyway, what difference would it make if she stopped herself from hearing what he had to say? None at all.

'Tell me,' she said, the words emerging as a barely there whisper when her throat was so tight it felt as if she was shouting. 'They've died, haven't they? My babies are dead.'

CHAPTER TEN

'JENNYWREN, no!' Daniel exclaimed, then shocked her completely by wrapping his arms around her in front of a roomful of fascinated staff.

For several heartbeats she allowed herself to absorb all the strength and warmth and security that Daniel was offering before she forced herself to pull back. Briefly, he resisted, but of course he was only trying to comfort her, wasn't he? That was *her* body trembling so hard, or was he shaking, too?

'They're *alive*, Jenny. Both of them…for the moment, at least,' he added ominously even as she was trying to absorb the fact that her worst nightmare hadn't happened.

How had she managed to miss hearing the sound of their heartbeats when the ultrasound was performed? Had she so convinced herself that there would be nothing to hear that she'd totally ignored it, along with everything else around her?

A little bubble of hope began to rise inside her until she looked up into those beautiful blue eyes and saw the shadows that spoke of bad news as clearly as words.

'T-tell me,' she said, her teeth suddenly chattering so hard it was a wonder he could understand her.

'They're struggling,' he said concisely. 'It sometimes

happens like that. For no apparent reason, everything suddenly becomes critical.'

She forced her foggy brain to work, to make sense of what he was saying and what it meant for her precious boys.

'Wh-when will you operate?' she demanded, refusing to even think about the possibility that there was nothing he could do to save them.

He hesitated and a rush of panic sent her pulse rate into orbit.

'P-please, Daniel, you *have* to operate.' She was openly begging, now, and she didn't care who was listening. 'You're the only one who can do it. You're the only one who can save my babies.'

He must have made some signal to the other staff to leave the room because suddenly they were alone but for the rhythmic sounds of the monitoring equipment.

'There's a problem,' he said, sounding strangely hesitant.

Impatiently, she interrupted, 'If there wasn't a problem, I wouldn't need the surgery to save my babies' lives.'

'That's not the problem I'm talking about.' He was almost eerily calm when she just wanted to scream with frustration that something wasn't already happening to get her ready for the procedure. It was her babies' only chance of life and it should be happening *now*. Daniel shouldn't be here, talking to her, he should be scrubbing and reviewing the scans and the—

'Jenny, I think I should have you transferred to another hospital for the surgery,' he announced bluntly. 'I've held off from talking to you about this—about anything to do with the babies and you and me—because you said you weren't ready, but they're *my* babies, too, and the ethics committee will be far from happy when they hear about that. It'd be a serious breach of the rules. I could even lose my job if I were to operate on—'

'*No!*' Jenny interrupted frantically. '*Please*, Daniel, as long as no one knows, there's no reason why you can't perform the ablation. The last thing I want, the last thing the *babies* need, is for someone other than you—someone not as good a surgeon as you—to do the surgery.'

She gathered her unravelling nerves together and lowered her voice, glancing across to make sure that no one had come back into the room; that no one could be listening. 'Apart from the fact that transferring me would take time they might not have, we've been careful not to give anyone any reason to think there's any connection between you and the babies, so without DNA analysis, no one could possibly know there's a conflicting personal connection. *Please*, Daniel, I'm begging you. I want *you* to do it. I trust you. I lo…'

At the very last second she managed to swallow the forbidden admission of her feelings for him. Not only was it inappropriate at this time and in this place, but in the circumstances it was something he definitely didn't need to know, not unless there was some small possibility that he might care for her, too; that the concern he showed so readily to all his patients was for her as well as the babies she was carrying.

Once the decision was made, it wasn't long before she was being positioned with the pale mound of her belly surrounded by dark green drapes and the frightening array of technology that would enable Daniel to identify and seal off the connecting blood vessels that were causing all the problems.

Her thoughts were whirling around inside her head, prayers for the success of the surgery and the survival of her babies mixed with overwhelming gratitude that Daniel had agreed to perform the procedure. It would have been wonderful if he could have been in two places at once— sitting beside her to hold her hand as well as operating on her—but at least she was surrounded by familiar members of staff, many of whom had become almost like a family to her.

'Not long, now,' Sally Long encouraged. 'He's just scrubbing.'

Jenny managed to smile at the registrar she'd first met when she was doing a rotation in NICU. The young woman had quickly gained a reputation for her skill at being able to thread hair-fine needles into minute baby veins, the result of her love of embroidery, she claimed.

With the organised chaos going on around her, everyone focusing on their particular task to make ready as quickly as possible, she felt strangely disconnected, almost as if she was watching everything through a glass screen. There was the byplay between the anaesthetist and one of the nurses, a wink from one that put a sparkle in the eyes of the other, the serious expression on another face as instruments were tallied and laid out in readiness then the door swung open by a broad shoulder as Daniel entered the room, his hands held up out of the way of contamination as he approached her.

From the other side of the room his eyes met hers over the top of his mask and even though they were all she could see of him, their dark intensity told her everything he was feeling—his apprehension for the two little lives she carried, his determination to do his best for them, his concern for her—and suddenly, the jumble of disparate thoughts colliding inside her head arranged themselves into a strange kind of logic that seemed to make everything frighteningly clear.

She loved Daniel, loved everything about him, and had

done so ever since she'd met him. In fact, she loved him so much that even if his suggestion that they marry had only been for the sake of the babies, she was willing to accept his offer if that meant he could be a part of her life.

'Sally?' She beckoned her colleague closer. 'Can I ask you a huge favour?'

Daniel threw his cap and gown in the laundry bin and slumped back against the nearest wall, suddenly shaking so hard that he wasn't certain that his legs would hold him up.

'I did it!' he whispered and closed his eyes to send up a heartfelt prayer of thanks that his skill had been equal to the task.

It had been even more complex than he'd expected and taken nearly twice as long because, with the placenta implanted low down on the front wall of the uterus, he'd had to introduce a second trocar to be able to get the laser in the right position to seal off the last of the blood vessels. The procedure had ended with drawing off some of the excess fluid around the recipient twin, but he wouldn't know how successful the procedure had been until the amount of fluid around the smaller twin started to increase, indicating that he was finally receiving his fair share of the blood supply.

'And that is always dependent on the trauma of the surgery not triggering premature labour,' he murmured, tempted to cross his fingers, but as that was something that they couldn't be sure about for days or even weeks, keeping them crossed that long would be a practical impossibility.

For now, all he could do was celebrate the fact that the surgery had gone as well as he could have hoped, with every single blood vessel that had previously joined the two babies now permanently sealed.

He was desperate to go and check on Jenny again, needing to see with his own eyes that she'd recovered well from the strain of the procedure, but it would probably be a good idea to take the time to climb under a shower before he did. That might help him to get himself under control before he blurted out something that he shouldn't while she was in such a vulnerable state.

'Daniel?' A brief knock on the changing room door was accompanied by the sleekly elegant head of the Registrar who'd been observing the procedure, today, and his heart leapt into his mouth.

'Is there a problem, Sally?' he demanded, thrusting head and arms back into the scrub top he'd only just removed while his heart rate spiked. 'Jenny's not bleeding, is she? She hasn't started having contractions, has she?'

'No, it's not Jenny…well, it is…really, but not because of the surgery.' She stopped abruptly, muttered something under her breath and blew out a huff of laughter. 'I'm making a real mess of this, only she asked me just before the procedure was about to begin, and—'

'Sally, slow down! Take a deep breath,' Daniel advised and gestured towards the long narrow bench against the wall. 'Sit down and start at the beginning. Someone asked you to do something for them?'

'Jenny did,' she nodded as she perched gingerly on the edge of the bench. 'And she asked me to make absolutely certain that I sent you in to see her immediately after the procedure was over.'

'She *what*?' Daniel blinked. Whatever he'd been expecting, it hadn't been that. 'Did she say why?'

Sally bit her lip and couldn't seem to make herself meet his eyes. He was just about ready to break a habit of a lifetime and shout at a junior member of staff when she finally spoke.

'I don't know how much she's told you about her situation,' she began, 'and I would feel really uncomfortable breaking a confidence, but she asked me to make some arrangements for her and then said she would need to see you.' She hesitated a moment, as though unsure whether to go on, then added in an eager rush, 'I'm not certain, but I think it's got something to do with the father of her babies. I think she's going to ask you to get in contact with him for her.'

'What, exactly, did she tell you?' he managed to ask calmly, bracing his shoulders against the wall in a semblance of calm composure when there was a tornado of thoughts whirling around inside him. His own career could be on the line if the fact that he'd taken advantage of one of his staff became common knowledge, to say nothing of the fact that he'd operated on her and the babies he'd given her.

'First, she swore me to secrecy, so you have to swear that you'll never tell anyone what I'm telling you. Ever!' She looked so fierce that he knew that if he didn't promise, he wouldn't find out what was going on.

'I promise that I won't break Jenny's confidence in you,' he said and she blinked then shook her head.

'That's not the same,' she objected.

'I know,' he agreed, hoping he sounded calmer than he felt, 'but I have to leave myself some leeway to enable me to speak to Jenny, but I do promise that whatever you tell me will never go further than the three of us. Is that good enough?'

'It will have to do, I suppose,' she said grudgingly. 'But...'

'What did she tell you?' he asked before she could avoid the topic again. 'What did she want you to do?'

'She asked me to organise the delivery of a selection of balloons from the concession in the main lobby. Then she gave me the message for you, to be delivered after the ablation was finished.'

Daniel managed to force himself to stay long enough to thank Sally, but even when he left her he wasn't able to hurry to Jenny's side because an icily controlled woman accosted him in the hallway.

'Dr Carterton, it's time we spoke,' Jenny's mother said abruptly.

For just a second Daniel was ashamed to admit that his knees knocked as he was catapulted back into his eleven-year-old self, the first time he was called in front of the headmistress accused of fighting by the very bullies who had cornered him and blacked his eye.

It didn't take long to remind himself that those days were long gone. These days he could give as good as he got.

'Dr Sinclair,' he replied politely, silently reminding himself that he had every intention of putting the woman in the position of mother-in-law as soon as possible, no matter what scheme Jenny might have cooked up with Sally Long. At least she'd come to find out how her daughter's surgery had gone. 'Shall we go to my office?'

'Here will do well enough,' she snapped, clearly incensed. 'I want the name of the man who dishonoured my family by getting my daughter pregnant, and you're going to give it to me.'

Her arrogant assurance that he would do what she said just because she'd said it meant that Daniel had to bite his tongue and count to ten to keep his anger under control. The fact that he hadn't immediately complied was enough to have the colour on her cheekbones darkening with her rising anger.

'For heaven's sake, she's already noticeably pregnant!' Jenny's mother exclaimed. 'She should have the man's ring on her finger by now; should have been married months ago so people could at least have pretended they didn't notice it was only a six-month pregnancy.'

'I'm sure she could have had the ring, *if* she wanted it,' Daniel said tersely, fuming that the woman seemed to care so little about Jenny's happiness. His Jennywren was worth far more than a cobbled-together marriage of convenience purely for social appearances. That was exactly why he hadn't badgered her to accept his proposal after she'd refused him, even though he ached to make her his. 'Any man would be lucky to have her as a wife,' he added, pushing his private ache to one side. 'She's beautiful, bright, caring, dedicated—'

'Well, if you think so highly of her, why don't *you* marry her?' she demanded impatiently. 'I'd make it worth your while.'

Daniel shook his head in disbelief. 'You obviously don't know your daughter at all, and you certainly don't know anything about *me* if you think I would accept a bribe to force her into a marriage she didn't want.' He gave a brief bark of laughter that was totally devoid of any humour. 'And to think I thought you'd come here to find out how the surgery had gone!'

'Surgery? What surgery?' she demanded before a hopeful smile spread over her face. 'Did she finally see sense and decide it was better to get rid of the baby?'

'Hardly!' Daniel snapped, almost incandescent with rage that the woman should think so little of those precious scraps of humanity, only subliminally aware that Jenny apparently hadn't even bothered to inform her parents that she was carrying twins, let alone that their lives were in danger.

Well, if she hadn't wanted to tell them, he certainly wasn't going to. The only thing that really mattered to him was that Jenny had asked to see him, and her mother was delaying him for her own selfish reasons.

'I've just had to perform *in utero* surgery to save two babies' lives. Now, if you'll excuse me, I'm sure you'll understand that I need to check up on my patients,' and he had absolutely no regrets that he hadn't told her that it was her daughter and her grandchildren that he was talking about.

His heart was in his mouth and his pulse was beating at twice its normal rate by the time he tapped on Jenny's door, all the possible reasons why she might have asked Sally to pass on her message jumbled in his head.

The only thing that shone like a clear beacon was his determination to try to persuade her that he loved her enough for both of them and if she would only agree to marry him, he would spend the rest of his life taking care of her and their babies.

He knew that the next few minutes were more crucial to his future than anything that had gone before and he was terrified because this was the first challenge in his life that he couldn't overcome by hard work and persistence alone.

'Come in,' called her familiar voice and his heart gave an extra kick in response, then kicked again when he saw the smile that greeted him when she saw him at the door.

His eyes drank in the sight of her greedily, noting that she was still a little pale after such a stressful time but that one hand was gently stroking the curve of her belly as though soothing her tiny passengers.

'Daniel!' She beckoned him in with the other hand but must have seen something in his face because her smile immediately vanished. 'What's the matter? Did something go wrong during the procedure? Did you find something that—?'

'No, Jenny!' he exclaimed, silently castigating himself for worrying her. He'd thought he had a better poker face than that, but perhaps Jenny was the one person who could see beyond that; to know with nothing more than a look that he had something on his mind. 'I had my doctor's head on, checking to see that you were all right. Nothing adverse to report? Nothing worrying you?'

'Nothing,' she agreed happily, settling herself deeper into her nest of pillows. 'I feel about a ton lighter now that weight has been taken off my shoulders. How soon did you say I could go home? And how soon will you be able to tell how successful the op's been, that the bigger twin's heart has recovered from the strain of coping with so much of the circulation?'

'And how many more questions are you going to fire at me without waiting for a single answer?' he teased as he hitched one hip onto the side of her bed and took her hand in his, careful of the drip he'd had left there as a precautionary measure, using it temporarily to deliver antibiotics to ward off the possibility of a post-operative infection.

'I'm sorry!' she laughed. 'Only, for the first time since you diagnosed the TTTS I feel as if I can really look forward to these two, to start to enjoy the whole process of pregnancy and—'

'Jennywren, can I ask you a question?' he interrupted, almost hating to break into her bubbly mood, but he'd been waiting and wanting her for such a long time and he couldn't wait any longer.

'Of course you can!' she exclaimed. 'You're my own personal miracle worker so you can ask anything you like. Anything at all!'

'In that case…' With his heart in his mouth he paused just long enough to capture her hand. 'Jenny Sinclair, will you marry me…please?'

* * *

'Marry you?' Jenny managed to reply before the power of speech completely deserted her.

Of *course* she wanted to marry him! That was the whole reason why she'd sent Sally Long to give him her message, but then he'd started asking how she was, as if he was only there to check up on a post-operative patient and she'd been distracted.

The suddenly unreadable expression on his face was enough to tell her that she'd paused too long, distracted by the conflicting thoughts colliding inside her brain and that her hesitation had hurt him—the one man who had never been anything but kind to her, who had proved over and over again that he cared for her without having to say a single word.

'Daniel…' There was nothing she'd love better than to be Daniel Carterton's wife, but she couldn't accept, not until she had the answers she needed. As soon as she'd seen his handsome face her heart had done a crazy happy dance in welcome, but in spite of the fact that this was the second time he'd proposed marriage, she didn't even know if he loved her, because he'd never said so…not once…and her pride didn't like the idea that the babies might be the only reason he was with her.

Obligation and duty were not the best reasons for two people to tie the knot. In fact, the only reason she would ever marry would be for love, and that would have to be to someone who not only loved her babies—the way soft-hearted Daniel loved all babies—but loved her just as much.

'Daniel…' she began again. The muddle inside her head and her heart were almost making her dizzy, and she certainly wasn't expecting him to surge to his feet as though he was going to leave her before she could find the words to ask him why he wanted her to marry him.

Except he didn't leave; simply straightened his shoulders and drew in a deep breath before he fixed her with a stern look that stilled everything inside her while she waited for him to speak.

'Well, then, it looks as if it's time to put my cards on the table,' he said, and she wondered if he realised that she could hear the slight tremor in his voice that told her he wasn't quite as resolute as he appeared.

'I know when you were trying to persuade me to do the surgery you said that there was no personal connection for the ethics committee to object to, but we both knew that wasn't true because they're my babies and also...' He snatched another breath and met her eyes straight on before he continued.

'Jenny Sinclair, I love you, in spite of the fact that you are probably the most stubborn female on God's green earth, and even if you weren't having my babies, I would still love you. So, will you please, *please*, say you'll marry me?'

For several endless seconds she felt as if she sat there with her mouth opening and closing like a goldfish, unable to find a single word to answer him as her heart turned somersaults inside her.

'You love me?' she finally managed to echo in disbelief.

'Of course I do,' he declared fiercely, reclaiming his place on the side of her bed and capturing both of her hands in the warm strength of his. 'I've been in love with you for months, almost since the day you walked into the unit and asked what extra training you would need to join my team.' His laughter had little humour in it. 'But I assumed with your family background that you were out of my league. I can't for one moment imagine that I'm your parents' ideal candidate for son-in-law!'

'Even though I'm not their natural daughter and have

been making my own choices since I was a teenager?' she interrupted wryly, tightening her grip on his clever fingers. 'Do you really think I would allow them to influence my choice of husband?'

'When you told Colin that you were adopted and therefore wouldn't inherit the family wealth, that was the first time that I allowed myself a glimmer of hope that someone from so far the other side of the tracks might stand a chance with you—that you weren't hung up on position and money. But it was the fact that you were pregnant with my babies that made me determined to try to change your mind about marriage, about me.'

'Ah, well, I might have been guilty of a little misrepresentation about the situation of my inheritance,' she admitted, hoping she wasn't just about to shoot herself in the foot.

'Misrepresentation? In what way?' He frowned.

'Well, by law, once you're adopted into someone's family, you become as much a part of that family as if you were a natural-born member, with all the same rights.'

'So, does that mean that you *will* be inheriting all that stuff?' His expression was growing darker by the second but it wasn't until he drew his hands away from hers completely that she started to panic.

'A house and a few fields? Yes, I could, if I wanted to,' she admitted, then deliberately took his hands back in hers. 'But that would only be after both my parents are gone and providing they hadn't got rid of it in the meantime.'

'Got rid of it?' he echoed, clearly amazed. 'Why?'

'For so many reasons.' She rolled her eyes. 'Because they're both workaholics who never spend any time there. Because it costs an absolute fortune to maintain—tens of thousands every year that can't possibly be covered by the rental that comes in from letting the fields out for grazing, or the income from letting occasional film crews use it for historic costume dramas, or as a venue for lavish weddings,' she enumerated. 'It might be different if Mum stayed at home to run everything to maximise the income—she's a brilliant organiser and would do it really well—but she'd go round the bend without her medicine.'

'So, what are they thinking of doing with it?' He was clearly intrigued, now. 'Obviously they can't just abandon such an historic place?'

'They've had several boutique hotel chains begging to be allowed to take it off their hands, but wouldn't make a decision until they saw me safely married off—perhaps, in case it spoiled my prospects? I think they were hoping I'd fall for the second son of one of the neighbouring estates, someone who wasn't in line to inherit a stately pile of his own but was accustomed to the lifestyle.'

'And as an independent woman living in London with a career you're unlikely to want to give up—'

'Except for the right incentives,' she interrupted, feeling it was past time they left the topic of her parents' hopes and wishes and got back to their own.

'And what incentives would they be?' he enquired, switching his focus every bit as quickly as she had.

She paused for a moment, as though in thought, but in truth she was taking pleasure in just looking at him, noting that the electric atmosphere between them was almost crackling with anticipation, and the extra gleam in those deep blue eyes reminded her of sunshine glinting off water.

'Well, if I were to marry, I would want it to be to someone who loved me—'

'I've already told you I do,' he interrupted, 'when I asked you to marry me.'

'He'd have to love me for *me*, not because I was carrying his children—'

'Would loving you even *more* because you're carrying my children count?' he interrupted again. 'Would loving you even more because you look more beautiful, more womanly, more sexy, more desirable with every day?' He punctuated each compliment with a kiss, the final one delivered on her parted lips.

It was several breath-stealing moments before he drew away again, just far enough to murmur in a voice roughened by emotion.

'Ah, Jennywen, don't you understand? The babies are a very welcome bonus, but the *only* reason I want to marry you is because I love you to distraction.'

He leant forward to kiss her again as though he was unable to resist and muttered under his breath when he became entangled in the strings of several balloons tied to the IV stand.

'What *is* this lot?' he demanded, trying to push them out of his way.

'What does it look like?' she asked with a chuckle and a glance up at the brightly coloured shapes bobbing silently above their heads.

The identical blue ones both bore the message 'It's a boy!' The silver one said 'Congratulations, Daddy!' The scarlet, heart-shaped one spoke for itself and the white one asked the simple handwritten question, 'Will you marry me?'

EPILOGUE

JENNY struggled to open her eyes, but she didn't need to be able to see to know whose arms were holding her so gently, yet so securely, and a tired but happy smile crept over her face.

'I'm sure you must be breaking at least a dozen hospital rules,' she managed in a voice husky with sleep.

'I don't think you'll find any rules that say a husband can't cuddle his wife to thank her after she's given him the two most beautiful sons in the world,' he said smugly, then pressed a kiss to the side of her face. 'How are you feeling?'

'As if I could sleep for a week,' she admitted. 'And as if I could run a marathon or float up to the ceiling like a balloon.'

'All at once?' he teased. 'Sounds exhausting.'

'Not as exhausting as carrying those two around that last fortnight,' she grumbled. 'Whoever said that babies are quieter the closer they get to the due date *lied*! They kick incessantly, day and night, and they never sleep, either.'

'So, how come you want to run a marathon and float round the room?' He helped her to slide up the bed just a little, knowing that the epidural wouldn't wear off for a while, yet.

'I could float because I suddenly feel as light as a

feather, *and* I can see my toes again! And I feel as if I could run a marathon because…well, I suppose it's the relief that they're finally here.'

'And relief that, after all the uncertainty, both Sam and Josh are a good weight and it looks as if we did the operation before any irreparable damage was done to Sam's heart.'

Jenny could remember all too clearly how tightly they'd clung to each other while they waited for the preliminary tests to be done on their precious newborn boys, almost unaware of the repair going on after the Caesarean that had been necessary to bring them into the world.

'How soon can I go up to the nursery to see them?' she demanded. 'I don't have to wait until I can walk, do I?'

'You know me better than that,' he chided. 'I wouldn't make you wait. I was just waiting until you were properly awake before I get some helpers in here. They're probably lined up in the corridor outside your door, hoping they'll get a chance to see our boys, too.'

Before he had a chance to do more than get his feet on the floor there was a sharp tap on the door and her father's head appeared.

'Ready for visitors?' he asked, then strode in without waiting for an answer, the very picture of health since he'd finally bowed to the inevitable several weeks ago and had the bypass surgery. Apparently, it had been his wife's accusation that he wouldn't be around to see his grandchildren that had made him see sense.

Then, during his recuperation, he'd realised that he rather loved the grand old house that had been passed down to him—and had been the venue for Jenny and Daniel's elegantly exclusive wedding—and with a bit of juggling of schedules, he could actually spend part of each week enjoying the gardens and overseeing the maintenance that would see the place in good enough repair to pass on to the next generation.

'When do we get our hands on our boys?' her mother said following close behind with a daintily wrapped parcel in her hands. 'There's a dragon in the nursery who wouldn't let us in, even though we're both consultants and we're their grandparents.'

It almost looked as if there was a hint of a blush on her cheeks as she handed the parcel over and Jenny was intrigued, quickly slipping off the elaborate blue bow and peeling back the paper covered in sleeping cherubs.

'Oh! They're beautiful!' she exclaimed when she saw the matched pair of pale blue cardigans, obviously hand-made rather than bought, and perfect in every stitch.

'I remembered that I rather enjoyed knitting for you when you were tiny,' her mother admitted, then added with a tone that was almost a challenge, 'I've decided that, since I'm cutting down on my hours in the hospital, too, I'm going to keep the babies in cardigans and jumpers. It will be up to you to tell me what they need and what colours you'd like me to use.'

Another tap at the door revealed Staff Nurse, clearly wanting the room cleared while she made Jenny's post-operative checks, and, with an unexpected hug from both of her parents and an admonishment to let them know as soon as they were allowed to visit the babies, they were gone.

'Do you want me to go, too?' Daniel asked, uncertain of the exact nursing protocols after a Caesarean now that he was on the parental side of the medical fence.

'Not at all,' Staff Nurse said with a wink. 'I thought it was probably the only way to persuade them to go so that you could take Jenny to the nursery to see the babies.'

'I can go now?' Jenny beamed. 'How am I going to get there—in a wheelchair?'

'You don't have to do a thing, just lie there and look beautiful,' Daniel said as he kicked off the brakes and began to manoeuvre the bed towards the doors that some-one out in the corridor had unlatched.

It felt almost like a royal procession by the time they reached the nursery, so many people had found an excuse to be there to congratulate them, but once Daniel and Jenny had used the hand sanitiser and gone through the doors they were virtually alone, curtains enclosing them with their two precious boys, even though only the top half of her bed could fit.

'Oh, Daniel, they're so perfect,' Jenny whispered, feeling the hot press of tears welling in her eyes. She'd had only the briefest glimpse of each of them as they were delivered. This was her first chance to feast her eyes on them.

'They are amazingly alike,' Daniel said ruefully. 'I can't see how we're ever going to be able to tell them apart. They're going to run rings round us when they get bigger.'

'It's easy enough at the moment,' Jenny pointed out, reaching one hand in to stroke one downy soft cheek then another, the two of them curled up side by side. 'Samuel Peter is the bigger one; Joshua Daniel still has some catching up to do.' She inspected as much as she could see of them, glad that the room was so warm that they only required nappies. It was easy to see how perfect they both were in every detail, then she started to chuckle.

'What's funny? What have you seen?' Daniel demanded.

'I've just spotted something that will give them away every time,' Jenny said triumphantly. 'Look at Sam's hair at the front. He's got a little cowlick, where the hair grows in a little clockwise whorl.'

It was Daniel's turn to chuckle. 'Josh has got the cowlick, too, but his is anticlockwise.'

'And if we don't tell them how we know which is which, by the time they work it out for themselves, we'll know the two of them and their different characters so well that we'll never get them muddled.'

'Ah, Jennywren, you're going to be such an awesome mother,' Daniel said suddenly, his expression very serious. 'How did I ever get so lucky?'

'I'm the lucky one,' she argued. 'I fell in love with the handsomest man in the hospital and all he seemed to want was to be my big brother.'

'When *I* didn't feel in the least bit brotherly,' he butted in, 'but if it was the only way I could spend time with you…'

'Then I seduced you and got pregnant, and you had to operate to save our babies' lives, and the rest is history,' she finished with a blissful smile.

'Oh, not history,' he disagreed, wrapping a loving arm around her shoulders and holding her so close that she could hear his heart beating, strong and true. 'That would mean it was over—in the past—and our lives together certainly aren't over. This is just the beginning of our own special happy-ever-after.'

* * * * *

SEPTEMBER 2011 HARDBACK TITLES

ROMANCE

The Kanellis Scandal	Michelle Reid
Monarch of the Sands	Sharon Kendrick
One Night in the Orient	Robyn Donald
His Poor Little Rich Girl	Melanie Milburne
The Sultan's Choice	Abby Green
The Return of the Stranger	Kate Walker
Girl in the Bedouin Tent	Annie West
Once Touched, Never Forgotten	Natasha Tate
Nice Girls Finish Last	Natalie Anderson
The Italian Next Door...	Anna Cleary
From Daredevil to Devoted Daddy	Barbara McMahon
Little Cowgirl Needs a Mum	Patricia Thayer
To Wed a Rancher	Myrna Mackenzie
Once Upon a Time in Tarrula	Jennie Adams
The Secret Princess	Jessica Hart
Blind Date Rivals	Nina Harrington
Cort Mason – Dr Delectable	Carol Marinelli
Survival Guide to Dating Your Boss	Fiona McArthur

HISTORICAL

The Lady Gambles	Carole Mortimer
Lady Rosabella's Ruse	Ann Lethbridge
The Viscount's Scandalous Return	Anne Ashley
The Viking's Touch	Joanna Fulford

MEDICAL ROMANCE™

Return of the Maverick	Sue MacKay
It Started with a Pregnancy	Scarlet Wilson
Italian Doctor, No Strings Attached	Kate Hardy
Miracle Times Two	Josie Metcalfe

MILLS BOON

SEPTEMBER 2011
LARGE PRINT TITLES

ROMANCE

Too Proud to be Bought	Sharon Kendrick
A Dark Sicilian Secret	Jane Porter
Prince of Scandal	Annie West
The Beautiful Widow	Helen Brooks
Rancher's Twins: Mum Needed	Barbara Hannay
The Baby Project	Susan Meier
Second Chance Baby	Susan Meier
Her Moment in the Spotlight	Nina Harrington

HISTORICAL

More Than a Mistress	Ann Lethbridge
The Return of Lord Conistone	Lucy Ashford
Sir Ashley's Mettlesome Match	Mary Nichols
The Conqueror's Lady	Terri Brisbin

MEDICAL ROMANCE™

Summer Seaside Wedding	Abigail Gordon
Reunited: A Miracle Marriage	Judy Campbell
The Man with the Locked Away Heart	Melanie Milburne
Socialite...or Nurse in a Million?	Molly Evans
St Piran's: The Brooding Heart Surgeon	Alison Roberts
Playboy Doctor to Doting Dad	Sue MacKay

Mills & Boon® Hard Back

October 2011

ROMANCE

HISTORICAL

MEDICAL ROMANCE™

0911 GEN STD HB

Mills & Boon® Large Print
October 2011

ROMANCE

HISTORICAL

MEDICAL ROMANCE™